PINEAPPLE

BEACH HOUSE

A Pineapple Port Mystery: Book Five

Amy Vansant

Vansant Creations, LLC / Amy Vansant
Annapolis, MD
http://www.AmyVansant.com
http://www.PineapplePort.com

Copy editing by Carolyn Steele.
Proofreading by Effrosyni Moschoudi & Connie Leap
Cover by Steven Novak

Dedication

To Brock, a sweet, snuggle-bear of a nephew-doggie who left   too   soon.

CHAPTER ONE

The tide rolled in, pushed by a tropical storm swirling off the North Carolina coast. The sea swallowed the beach, churning toward the colorfully painted houses that peered over the dunes, powerless to stop their approaching guest.

Even the most stalwart dunes meant little to an ocean once it decided to make a house call.

The tide served as a scout for the body of the storm. The wind had yet to arrive. A chill had fallen over the barrier island, but the center of the tempest spun hundreds of miles away, idling over the Atlantic Ocean, building strength.

The man and the woman on the porch, enjoying the last of the calm weather, didn't see the tendrils of water seeping through the ground beneath the sand.

As unstoppable as an army of ants.

More powerful than a train.

The trick was patience. The water had nothing to do but *rub*. Break. Move. Fill.

Fresh, salt, brackish—it didn't matter.

Water always won.

Things rise from the ground as the water displaces them from the places they've slept for years. Old pathway pavers, hidden by dirt for decades, shimmy their way to the surface when the water visits. Shells. Bricks. Bottles. Chunks of asphalt.

Bones.

Old and new.

Perched atop a nearby dune, a squirrel dug a hole and

dropped a trophy inside.

The man and the woman didn't see this happening from their spot on the porch.

But the ghost crabs smelled it.

CHAPTER TWO

"You've got to be kidding me."

Charlotte stared at herself in the mirrored doors of Mariska's closet. She wore a yellowing cream velvet dress cinched tight at the waist with a scoop neck collar and lace gloves.

In Florida.

Just looking at her outfit made her want to sweat.

Mariska whirled, her dark maroon cape spinning, knocking her deodorant, a hair brush, and a can of shaving cream to the floor.

"Oh, come on, this is fun," said Mariska, trying to bend and pick up the items that had fallen. Her dress wouldn't allow it.

Charlotte dipped to retrieve the items.

Mariska and Darla had been invited to a gothic romance

book party by Veronica Deering, one of the Pineapple Port ladies. They'd insisted that Charlotte join them.

Growing up as an orphan unofficially adopted by the Pineapple Port retirement community, Charlotte had been forced or cajoled into attending hundreds of ladies' book club meetings. Most of the time, she didn't mind. She knew book club meetings could be a *hoot* and were usually little more than an excuse to drink. Occasionally, it helped to *read* the featured book, but it was rarely required. Once or twice, she'd been asked to bring a potluck snack. But *no one* had ever requested she dress like undead Jane Eyre before.

"Leave it to Veronica to come up with this," said Charlotte, scratching where the lace irritated her neck.

"She's a little weird," agreed Darla.

Darla wore what Charlotte had referred to as a *Martha-Washington-as-professional-escort* ensemble. The costume shop had been woefully short on gothic romance dresses. If Veronica had requested they dress like pirate wenches, they would have had *scads* of outfits to choose from, though bare midriffs and plunging necklines in a fifty-five-plus community provided challenges of their own.

This she knew all too well.

Pirate wench outfits wouldn't do for this party, but it had still taken Charlotte ten minutes to talk Mariska out of buying a stuffed parrot to wear on her shoulder.

The three of them waddled to the lanai in their uncomfortable frocks to unveil their costumes to Mariska's husband, Bob, Darla's husband, Sheriff Frank, and Charlotte's boyfriend, Declan.

This was the part Charlotte had been dreading the most.

As they jostled through the sliding door that separated the lanai from the living room, Charlotte noticed the bourbons the men had poured in anticipation of their departure. The ladies' book club meant an impromptu meeting of their

Bourbon Club, the less-veiled version of the men's "book club."

"What do you think?" Mariska asked Bob as she completed a spin. Her cape clipped a small lamp, and Charlotte dove to catch it before it crashed to the ground.

"You look like vampire Mary Poppins," said her husband. He snorted at his own joke.

Frank eyeballed Darla. "You look like the inside of a coffin."

He flinched as Darla smacked him on the shoulder.

Charlotte hooked her mouth, glaring at Declan, awaiting his verdict.

He smiled. "You look lovely..."

She scowled. "Go ahead. Finish. Get it out of your system."

"...Miss Havisham."

Charlotte sighed. She knew she *did* look like Dickens' attic-dwelling abandoned bride. "I think her dress itched less than mine," she said, clawing again at her irritated neck.

Mariska shook a finger at Bob. "Don't drink too much. We don't want to come home to a bunch of idiots."

The three men looked at each other as if they couldn't imagine what she meant.

Assured no compliments would be forthcoming, the ladies shuffled toward the front door. Charlotte exited first and then turned in time to watch Mariska forcibly jerk Darla and her impressive poofs through the doorframe.

"A few more ruffles, and you would have had to grease me like a pig," said Darla.

Charlotte continued down the driveway, only to find herself confronted by Mariska's Volkswagen Bug. She put her hands on her hips and considered the physics of the task that lay before them.

"We're going to look like clowns stuffing ourselves in that thing."

"Let's take the golf cart," suggested Darla.

"The golf cart? That's even *smaller*," said Mariska.

"Yeah, but all our dangly bits can hang over the edges."

"Don't they always?" asked Mariska.

The two older ladies burst into giggles.

Charlotte frowned at the golf cart and decided there was *some* logic to Mariska's plan. She waddled to it.

They piled onto the cart, Mariska wedged behind the wheel with Darla beside her on the front bench. Charlotte, as usual, sat in the reverse rumble seat, clinging to the framework like a koala in a eucalyptus tree during a hurricane.

Mariska backed out of the driveway as if she were being chased by a mob of angry zombies, paused long enough for Charlotte to wrap her arm snake-like around the roof pole, and then stomped on the pedal.

Charlotte's knuckles turned white. Back when her real grandmother died and Mariska explained that she and the rest of the Pineapple Port retirement community would be raising her, she never dreamed how harrowing growing up in a fifty-five-plus neighborhood would be.

Mariska's cape unfurled and fluttered across Charlotte's face, slapping her as if demanding a duel. She wrestled it down and braced her feet as Mariska rolled left.

Veronica lived in the older part of Pineapple Port, but it didn't take long to arrive with Lead Foot at the wheel. Mariska screeched to a halt behind several other carts and cars. No matter how fast Mariska had driven, it appeared that stuffing their bodies into their costumes had still left them fashionably late.

The ladies piled from the golf cart and toddled to the house, muttering beneath their breaths as they repeatedly stepped on their own, and each other's, skirts.

Hostess Veronica Deering opened her door before they could knock. She was a tall woman with black hair and a matching skin-tight gown that made her look like Dracula's mistress. She grinned upon seeing them.

"Ladies, how good of you to come."

Mariska and Darla said their hellos. Charlotte also returned the greeting but felt her smile fading as her attention locked on Veronica's ruby-red lips.

Something about her shade of lipstick seemed *off*.

Too red? Too shiny?

Mariska noticed as well, gushing over the lip gloss. "Your lipstick almost looks like wet blood, but in a *good* way."

"You're too funny," said Veronica, chortling as she led them into the house. If she was offended by the comparison of her lip gloss to bodily fluids, she didn't show it. There was no denying that Mariska had perfectly articulated what Charlotte had been thinking.

The center island of Veronica's kitchen was laden with snacks. Mariska and Darla headed toward them as if pulled by magnets.

"I hope the deviled eggs aren't all gone," mumbled Mariska, straining to see.

A man nodded at Charlotte, and she smiled. He licked his lips, gazing at her as if he were starving and she was a juicy hamburger.

Hm. Disturbing.

Her progress toward the island grew slower, and she scanned the room, carefully avoiding eye contact with the leering man.

Oh no.

All the party guests appeared as if they'd just awoken from their coffins. Women in dresses with draping sleeves chatted with men in leather pants and frilly white shirts. *Seventy-year-old men in leather pants.* Several of the men wore eyeliner.

Charlotte scooted to Darla's side. "Notice anything odd

about this party?"

"Hm?" grunted Darla, a piece of pepperoni hanging from her lip for a second before her tongue swept it to safety.

"Look."

Charlotte grabbed Darla's head and pointed her gaze toward a man and a woman on Veronica's lanai. The man was licking the woman's neck.

Darla's eyes grew wide. "What in the name of fat Elvis are *they* doin'?"

Charlotte leaned past Darla to tug on Mariska's sleeve.

"Oh, Charlotte. You have to try this punch. It has the strangest consistency, and it's a little salty, but—"

"*Mariska*," Charlotte hissed. "What kind of party did you say this is?"

"Gothic romance?"

"What did Veronica call it, *exactly*?"

Mariska pursed her lips. "Um...just what I said. A Goth party."

Charlotte closed her eyes and groaned.

A steel-haired woman in a knee brace hobbled by sporting five earring piercings, a nose ring, a lip bolt, and what looked like a silver snake weaving through her eyebrow.

Darla gasped.

"Not something you see every day," agreed Charlotte.

"It's her *knee*."

Something about Darla's comment struck Charlotte as odd. "Wait... She just walked by with all those piercings and you gasped at her knee brace?"

Darla nodded. "You have to remove everything metal for an MRI. It must have taken her a *year* to get ready for it."

"And they're just the piercings we can *see*," said Mariska. She popped a cheese square into her mouth and stared at the crowd. "It looks like they're remaking the Golden Girls using the cast of the Addams Family."

Charlotte felt something brush her neck and jumped, yipping like a Yorkshire terrier. She whirled to find a tall, thin old man behind her, smirking. Slapping her hand to her neck, she felt *moisture.*

"Did you just lick my neck?" she asked, horrified.

His smile broadened, revealing what looked like pointy, filed-down dentures.

"Delicious," he said, his eyes flashing with import.

The man leaned towards her again, and she put her hand on his chest to stop his progress. She stared into his eyes.

"Buddy, you lick me again, and I'll drive a *porterhouse* steak through your heart. Believe me. It takes a lot longer to die that way."

The man blanched and wandered away.

Charlotte turned to Mariska and Darla.

"We're out of here," she said, circling her finger in the air above her head.

Darla and Mariska gathered a few extra snacks from the spread and followed her lead to the door.

"Are you leaving?" asked Veronica, touching Mariska's arm as she passed.

Mariska nodded. "There's been a mistake, Ronnie. I thought this was a *book* club."

Veronica gaped. "A *book club*? You know, I thought it was strange when you asked to come. What did you think *light S & M* meant on the invite?"

Mariska shrugged. "Snacks and meats?"

"Weirdos!" called Darla from the entrance landing. She leaned in and yanked Mariska outside.

Charlotte flashed Veronica an apologetic smile and hurried after the others.

The three of them crowded back into the golf cart, and Mariska hit the gas.

"Snacks and meats?" screamed Charlotte from the back.

Mariska glanced back at her. "How was I supposed to know that sort of thing was going on in Pineapple Port?"

"No telling the men. I'll never hear the end of it," said Darla.

Mariska nodded. "Absolutely. No telling."

Charlotte squelched her rising giggles and tried to remain quiet.

She couldn't *wait* to get back and tell Declan.

CHAPTER THREE

"It looked like a *True Blood* cast reunion party fifty years later."

Charlotte leaned on the checkout counter of Declan's pawn shop, the Hock o'Bell, sharing horror stories of the previous evening's *mature* goth party.

Shuffling through his *SALE!* tags, Declan hooted with laughter. "They have parties like that? I mean, in *that* neighborhood?"

"I guess so. I had no idea. And I've been here forever. I'm just sorry I missed the best part. Mariska said she asked Bob what *S and M* stood for, and he nearly choked on his coffee."

"You're a private investigator now. Shouldn't you have solved that puzzle before you had your neck licked?"

"I'm not official yet," said Charlotte. She'd completed the intern hours required to earn her official private investigator's license and submitted the paperwork. Now she had to wait. She was giddy at the idea of hanging her shingle. She could advertise her services without breaking the law. She could *finally* stop solving cases on the sly.

"So you're saying that if you'd *had* your license, you would have known all about the geriatric dungeon in your midst."

She nodded. "Naturally. What are you doing with all those sale tags? Are you having a sale?"

"Good guess, Sherlock. But no, as a matter of fact, I'm just counting them. I don't need to have sales anymore. These are the tags from items Blade sold yesterday. The man is a *machine*."

Declan's employee, Blade, stood at the front of the shop, chatting with an elderly woman as if they were long-lost friends. His six-foot-six frame, long gray-blond ponytail, weathered face, and exclusive wardrobe of war and death-related t-shirts made him a terrifying sight to behold, but the people of Charity, Florida, couldn't stop buying things from him.

Declan waved his hand in Blade's direction. "Look at that mustache. He's *terrifying,* and these people love him. Meanwhile, I can't shake the feeling he's selling all my taxidermy to make room for a stuffed *me*."

Charlotte twisted to survey Blade's new mustache. From beneath his nose, the blond streak spilled in straight lines down either side of his mouth like twin caterpillars agreeing to go their separate ways.

"You can't judge a book by its cover," she said.

"He made himself even *scarier* and had his best day ever. I think the locals buy things just to talk to him. Getting him to say more than three words a day to me is like pulling teeth. But everyone else—men, women, children—to them, he's like the pied piper of pawn."

Charlotte beheld her boyfriend's wistful expression. Declan was handsome, built like an Olympic swimmer, and *had* been the local ladies' obsession before Blade appeared.

"Jealous?" she asked.

He scoffed. "*No.*"

She patted his hand. "Aw. I still think you're cute."

"Gee, thanks."

She decided to change the subject. "So, are you ready for our vacation?"

Darla had friends, Phil and Brenda Scott, who owned a vacation home on the Outer Banks of North Carolina. The Scotts' rental home needed maintenance, and they'd offered to allow Darla and a group of her friends to stay for free over the Thanksgiving holiday in return for repairs. Sheriff Frank couldn't take the time off, so Darla invited Mariska and Bob, who considered himself handy. They'd invited Charlotte and Declan to join to gain access to their "strong young backs," and—never to be left out—Declan's uncle Seamus had weaseled his way into the group by promising to provide free transportation. Mariska completed the list by inviting her sister Carolina, who lived in Michigan. Her husband, Chuck, was an electrician, so he made for a useful addition.

The plan was for Carolina and Chuck to fly to the nearest airport and rent a car while the Florida crew drove north in whatever vehicle Seamus provided.

Declan wrapped the *SALE!* tags in a rubber band and threw them in a drawer. "I'm still not convinced driving north in November to stay in the middle of nowhere in the freezing cold is a *vacation*."

"Oh, come on. It will be fun. How handy are you?"

"Not at all. But Seamus is. He's always fixing things around the house. That's the only reason I didn't tackle him when he opened his mouth and invited himself."

Charlotte smiled. "Ah. That explains why you haven't changed your locks. He'd just change them back."

Seamus had been living with Declan since returning to Charity from Miami several months earlier. If Declan dropped any more hints suggesting Seamus find a place of his own, they wouldn't be able to walk through the living room for tripping over them.

Seamus worked on *Seamus time*. But as a private

investigator, he'd been able to help Charlotte earn hours towards her detective's license, so she owed him.

Charlotte sensed movement behind her and hopped away in time to avoid an approaching deer antler.

"Sorry, Miss Charlotte," said Blade in his husky baritone as he hefted a mounted deer head onto the counter. There was an eye patch slung over the stuffed creature's left eye, giving it a rakish expression.

An elderly couple, transfixed on the deer and seemingly luminous with glee, trailed behind Blade.

Blade sniffed. "You want me to ring it up?"

Declan stared at the head, his jaw slack. He snapped to attention at the sound of Blade's question.

"Huh? No, I've got it. Thank you, Blade."

Declan rang up the couple's prize.

"You never showed us this before," said the woman to Declan in an accusatory tone.

He looked up from the credit card machine. "The deer?"

She nodded.

"Mrs. Whitmore, that deer has been hanging on the shop wall since I was a little kid."

The woman shook her head as if she didn't believe him.

"That can't be right," said her husband.

"No," she agreed.

Declan handed her back her card. "I swear. All Blade did was put an eye patch on it."

"Well, it was *genius*." Mrs. Whitmore turned and beamed at Blade, who grinned back, his mustache stretching twice its length to complete the feat.

Declan scowled as Blade hefted the head and carried it to the car for the Whitmores. The shop bell jingled as he wrestled it through the front door.

"I swear, that thing has been here since I got the place," said Declan to Charlotte the moment the door closed.

"I believe you."

"That makes one of you."

"Why, exactly, did it have a patch over its eye?"

"That was Blade's idea. One glass eye was cracked, so he put a patch over it. He's been introducing it to the customers as Blackdeer'd."

Charlotte laughed. "You have to admit. The man's a retail genius."

"Oh, shut *up*." Declan snatched his shop keys from the counter and headed for the door. "Let's get out of here."

In the parking lot, Declan handed the keys to Blade as the big man headed back toward the shop.

"I'll be back in a week. If you need anything, you've got my number."

Blade nodded and winked at Charlotte. "Hey, when you get back, Miss Charlotte, remind me to tell you the story of Blackdeer'd, the most fearsome forest pirate in the world."

Charlotte nodded. "Wouldn't miss it for the world. You'll have to find a new store mascot now."

He motioned to the store. "There's a black-tailed deer in the back. I'm going to bring him out and get him a top hat and bow tie."

"Ha. Black-tailed. I get it. Have a name for him? How about instead of Fred Astaire, call him Fred A*stag*?"

"Perfect." Blade held up a hand, and they high-fived.

Declan headed for his car, muttering to himself as Charlotte jogged after him. She hopped in the passenger seat, still chuckling at his irritation.

"That Blade. He is just the most charming—"

Declan started his car. "Yeah, yeah, yeah. Very funny."

"I guess we need to go to your house and get your bag?"

He shook his head. "I have a bag packed in the back seat."

"Perfect."

As they made the short drive to Pineapple Port to meet

the others, Charlotte listed the things she remembered from the North Carolina to-do list. "We're supposed to paint, and I think there's a bad drain—"

"What is *that*?" asked Declan as they pulled onto the street where Mariska, Darla, and Charlotte lived.

Charlotte scowled. "What's a *drain*?"

"No, *that*." He pointed out the windshield.

Charlotte spotted an enormous Day-Glo green bus parked *literally* on the curb outside Mariska's house. Whoever had parked it hadn't stopped in time, and it sat listing to the left like a ship run aground.

The hood of the bus was emblazoned with a snake's face, complete with poison-tipped fangs. Large, yellow eyes stared back at them as they gaped at the vehicle.

"It's a modified school bus," said Declan, his voice dropping to an awed whisper as they coasted toward the strange machine.

Declan chose not to pull in to Charlotte's driveway and instead rolled past the bus so they could survey the full length.

"Are those *scales*?" asked Charlotte.

A snake-scale pattern covered the body of the bus with *The Reptile* scrawled in 3-D, blood-red letters.

Mariska, Bob, Darla, and Seamus milled around the back of the vehicle. They waved as Charlotte and Declan arrived beside them.

"Please don't tell me that's our ride to North Carolina," said Declan, putting his car in park. He rested his head on the steering wheel and muttered one word.

"Seamus."

Charlotte stepped out of the car and stared at *The Reptile's* enormous wheels.

"We're going to have to haul you ladies into that thing with a crane," she said.

"We can get in just fine. Go get your suitcase," said Darla.

Charlotte jogged back to her house to retrieve her luggage and Abby, her soft-coated wheaten terrier, who'd been granted the thumbs up to join in. She locked the door and saw Declan had parked his car in her driveway before returning to the bus.

She returned to *The Reptile,* bag and leash in hand.

"Oh, I'm so glad you're here. Let's go. Let's go!" said Mariska, herding the others toward the bus like a sheepdog.

"Where did you get this thing?" asked Charlotte.

Mariska clasped her hands together. "Remember when I said it would be great to find a car that could fit *all* of us?"

"Yes. Though I have to admit, at the time, I was thinking a *van,* not a giant mechanical snake bus."

"That's what I thought, too, but vans wouldn't do. The house can only be reached by driving on the beach, so we needed something that could make it through the sand."

"You mean there's no road to the house?"

Mariska shook her head. "Just the beach. Isn't that exciting?"

"I guess. But vans can't get there?"

"Vans sink in the sand. We needed something with big tires."

Charlotte kicked one of *The Reptile's* tires. "I think we're safe. But how—"

"I have an old buddy who offered to let us borrow his baby," said Seamus, appearing at her side.

Charlotte raised an eyebrow. "He didn't have any cars to crush this weekend?"

Seamus shook his head. "My dear girl. *The Reptile* doesn't crush cars. She's totally street legal."

"She?"

"Of course. She's a snake."

"Watch it, buster."

Seamus laughed and pretended to cower as Charlotte

held up a fist.

"Let's go!" screamed Darla from somewhere on the other side of the bus.

Charlotte circled the vehicle to find Declan with the others.

"We have to film them trying to get into this thing," she said.

He held up his phone. "Already on it."

Seamus lifted a panel and pulled a lever hidden in the side of the bus. The doors opened and a set of stairs folded out.

Charlotte pouted. The stairs would make it easy for everyone to enter. "Well, that's no fun."

Declan slipped his phone back into his pocket.

One by one, they climbed the stairs into the belly of the snake, each doing his or her best to arrange their bags and sit without stepping on Darla's miniature dachshund, Turbo, as he tore up and down the center aisle. Mariska and Bob's dog, Izzy, a Dalmatian mutt that looked more like a short, stout pillow stuffed to bursting, stared at Mariska until she agreed to lift her onto the seat with Bob's help.

Bob announced that he would take the first shift and claimed the driver's seat.

Declan threw their luggage into the back seat, dodging Turbo as he made his laps. The miniature dachshund whipped under the seats and appeared a moment later to run headlong into his shins. The puppy shook off the collision and bolted away again.

Charlotte noticed an enormous cooler stowed in the back. "What's in the cooler? Please say *road snacks*."

"That's the turkey," said Mariska.

"You're bringing the Thanksgiving turkey to North Carolina?"

Mariska nodded. "And all the trimmings. I don't know if they have it all up there."

Charlotte frowned. "We're going to North Carolina, not the jungles of South America."

"Though you wouldn't know it from our mode of transportation," mumbled Declan.

Mariska shrugged. "You never know."

Abby hopped on the seat beside Charlotte, wedging her furry butt between her mommy and Declan on the bench-style seating.

"Ready?" Charlotte asked, reaching past the dog to pat Declan on the knee.

Ooof! was all he said in response as Abby collapsed into his lap.

Declan tried to shift out from under Abby's pointy elbows, but unhappy to be moved, she only leaned *harder* against him. She inched him off the end of the seat until he was hanging by one butt cheek.

Declan gave up and moved to the seat across the aisle. Abby stretched out to enjoy her hard-won space.

"Sorry," said Charlotte.

Declan leaned back. "Don't worry. I know the pecking order."

"She comes before me, too, so I know how you feel."

Declan chuckled. "You know, sometimes I think about how boring my life was before I met you, and I just want to cry."

She grinned. "Are you saying you *haven't* ridden in a snake bus before?"

CHAPTER FOUR

Charlotte checked the weather on her phone. Living in Florida, she'd grown accustomed to assuming every day would be sunny until it rained in the late afternoon. It took her until Georgia to realize North Carolina might not be just *colder* but maybe less predictable.

She stared at her phone, trying to reconcile the blobs of color there. The weather app displayed two enormous bands, one blue and one red and yellow, headed for a collision somewhere over North Carolina.

That can't be right.

She played the animation over again.

Same thing.

When she played the "future" animation, the icy blue blob heading east from the Midwest ran directly into the arms of an enormous, throbbing multicolored splotch approaching from the Atlantic Ocean. All signs pointed to the systems having their tête-à-tête in the living room of their North Carolina rental home, give or take a few feet.

The splotch looked vaguely *hurricane-y*.

Hurricanes, she knew.

"Hey, Mariska, did you happen to check the forecast this

morning?"

Mariska turned and offered her a blank stare.

Charlotte knew what that meant. *Everyone* had taken the weather for granted. The weather was so consistently hot in Florida, and the afternoon rain storms so predictable; that, barring hurricanes, people tended to forget weather existed.

She held up her phone, though she knew there was no chance Mariska could see the screen from her seat at the front of the bus. "There's an enormous cold front and a giant storm on a collision course over Corolla."

Mariska shrugged and returned her attention to the road. "Lucky we're going to North Carolina."

Charlotte dropped her phone to her side and stared at the back of Mariska's head.

"Mariska?"

"Hm?"

"*Corolla* is the city where we're staying in North Carolina."

Mariska twisted to face her again. "I thought we were going to Duck?"

"They used to live in Duck. They bought the Corolla house two years ago," said Darla without glancing up from the book she was reading.

Mariska's expression fell even further. "Really? I wanted to stay in a town called Duck. That just sounds *adorable*."

"Right now, it just sounds *wet*," muttered Charlotte. She peered at her phone again, flipping through a few more screens, deftly dodging ads that promised to show her the top ten strangest things Tornados had dropped in people's yards.

She sighed. "I can't figure out what's going to win—the snow or the storm. Either way, it's bad for us. Are you sure Carolina and Chuck made it out of Michigan? They might be snowbound."

Mariska shook her head. "They're already at the beach

house. The flights were cheaper two days earlier. Brenda almost had a conniption when I told her Carolina would be there early. I guess she had to call her rental service to put the key under the mat sooner than she'd planned."

"So I should expect everything done by the time we get there?" asked Charlotte.

"Nooo... But Carolina *did* do all the shopping for us, food *and* supplies."

"That's good. We should try to get there before the storm hits. No delays, no unscheduled stops—"

"I have to piddle," announced Darla, slapping her book on the seat next to her.

Charlotte scowled. "We just stopped fifteen minutes ago."

"Can't help it. Old bladder plus two cups of coffee equals *piddle*. It's simple math."

"But every time we make a pit stop, you get another cup of coffee."

"It's a *rest* stop. I'm required by law to get coffee, so I have a good reason to visit the *next* rest stop. It's the cycle of life."

"I have to go, too," said Mariska.

Charlotte rubbed her temples. "We're going to be able to trade this bus in for a flying car by the time we get there. It will be *that far in the future.*"

She looked out the window and watched the gaping stares of motorists stunned by *The Reptile* before slouching down in her seat.

"Do you have to go?" asked Darla as they pulled off Interstate 95 and into another rest stop.

Charlotte shook her head. "I'll walk the dogs."

Declan stood. "I'll help. I could use a leg stretch."

They piled off the bus, and Charlotte and Declan led the three dogs into the small forest that ran along the edge of the rest stop.

They were only a few feet into the trees when Turbo started barking.

Charlotte scowled. "That's weird. He never barks."

"Look!"

Declan pointed, and Charlotte followed his direction to discover a creature sitting on its haunches, staring back at them and rubbing his hands like a little bandit.

"A raccoon!"

·   Turbo released a steady stream of staccato yaps. Charlotte crouched down and pulled the dogs close to her. "I hope it isn't rabid or something. Get between us."

Declan looked at her. "Did you just ask me to act as the last line of defense between you and a rabid raccoon?"

She nodded. "There are four of us. It's only fair."

Declan grimaced. "Boy, you're lucky you're cute." He waved his arms at the animal. "Shoo!"

The raccoon walked away a few steps, paused, and then glanced back at Declan. It seemed to Charlotte that the animal couldn't decide whether it could take Declan in a fight or not, and the debate was still up for discussion in its little furry head.

Declan stomped, and the raccoon decided he was outmatched. It left, though unhurried and with plenty of attitude.

When it was out of sight, Turbo stopped barking.

"Who knew wiener dogs hate raccoons?" said Charlotte.

"I can't say I love them either," said Declan.

"What happened?" asked Darla, appearing behind them, out of breath.

"We were confronted by a cocky raccoon," said Charlotte. "He left."

Darla scooped up Turbo. "He never barks. I was afraid something happened to y'all."

They loaded on the bus and drove for another ten

minutes before Darla threw back her head with an exasperated huff.

"Oh *no*."

"What's the matter?" asked Charlotte.

"I heard Turbo barking and came running."

"I know. I was there."

She turned and looked at Charlotte. "I forgot to go to the bathroom."

Six rest stops and six cups of coffee later, they reached Duck, North Carolina, as the first snowflakes began to fall. It was Seamus' turn at the wheel, so he activated the forked-tongue-shaped windshield wipers as they wheeled onto the ramp that led to the beach and then headed north to Corolla.

The waves that flanked their right were large and churning, crashing to the sand as if trying to pound it into glass. Charlotte shimmied past Abby to Declan's side of the bus and stared out at the dark horizon hovering beyond the sea.

"Watch for horses," said Darla.

Seamus glanced back at her from his perch at the wheel. "Sea horses?"

"More like Sea *Biscuits*. Horses with hooves. Brenda said there are wild ones roaming around up here."

After one missed turn and one U-turn, they spotted the house, pulled off the beach, and parked in the driveway.

They disembarked as the snow began to fall. Charlotte and Declan took the dogs inside and then returned to grab the food and luggage. The snow was turning into stinging sleet, and they wanted to get everything inside as soon as possible.

Charlotte scanned the area as she waited for Seamus to open the back. In an upper window of the house next door, she spotted a face peering down at them. She imagined the neighbor was less interested in them than in their enormous, scale-covered snake bus.

She waved, and the figure waved back.

Seamus popped open the back door, and they dragged what they could carry into the large wood-shingled house. By the time the last bags were inside, the sleet had once again turned to snow.

Figures.

Mariska's sister, Carolina, stood at the front door looking flustered as Charlotte carried the last of the bags up the tall staircase that led to the front door. The house was built on stilts, with a smaller enclosed area beneath the main level.

"I almost called the cops when you pulled up," said Carolina, scowling at the bus. "You looked like a lost rock band. I thought you'd come to kill us."

"Why would a rock band want to kill you?" asked Charlotte.

Carolina rolled her eyes. "They're all on *the drugs*. You never know."

Charlotte smirked at Declan. "They're all on *the drugs*," she whispered.

Declan nodded. "They're the worst kind."

"Is that one of those Vipers?" asked Chuck, joining Carolina in the entryway. "I pictured them more sporty-like."

Mariska hugged Carolina, who grimaced and grew stiff as a board as she submitted to her sister's affections.

Mariska didn't seem to notice. "Did you get here okay? Any trouble?"

Carolina's permanent scowl found another gear. "Why would you stay in a place that you have to drive on the *sand* to get to? We practically had to buy a camel." She pointed a finger in the direction of the Jeep they'd rented, her expression implying that it might be an alien life form.

Mariska clucked her tongue. "I told you we didn't rent this place. It's *free* in exchange for a little handyman work. Isn't it lovely here? Did you see horses?"

"We saw neighbors. That place over there is full of old people." She bounced her head in the direction of the house next door.

"What do you mean?" asked Mariska, tilting to see around her sister.

"You know, where they put people when they get old."

"You mean it's a nursing home?"

Carolina shrugged. "Let's just say no one over there is winning the hundred-meter dash any time soon."

Charlotte took a moment to study the neighbor's house again. Beside the front door, she spotted a carved and painted sign that said *Elder Care-o-lina.*

"It's called the *Elder Care-o-lina.* That's cute," she said.

Carolina grunted.

Charlotte chuckled and took advantage of the lull in complaining to hug Chuck and Carolina. When she'd finished, she displayed a hand in Declan's direction.

"Carolina, you remember Declan."

Carolina nodded and turned her back to him. She took a step back, boxing Declan away as she leaned to whisper into Charlotte's ear.

"Where's he sleeping?" she asked.

CHAPTER FIVE

Declan threw his bag at the foot of the bed.

"I don't know. Are you *sure* it's okay if we share a room? Carolina didn't seem very happy about the idea."

Charlotte rolled her eyes. "We're twenty-six years old. Not sixteen."

"I know, but—"

She took his hand. "It's okay. I already talked to Mariska about it. There are five bedrooms and five couples—if you count Seamus as a couple."

"I could sleep on a couch."

"It's okay, I *swear*. They know having everyone in this house is more of a hanky-panky deterrent than a welded chastity belt."

"No kidding. But...wait. Did you just say hanky-panky? I think that is more of a deterrent than anything else."

Charlotte chuckled. "Seriously, it's—"

A scream rang out. They froze, staring at each other for a moment before Charlotte bolted for the door with Declan on her heels.

"That was fast," she said as they hit the stairs.

"What? You know what it is?"

"No, but I knew *something* had to happen."

As they reached the main floor, they paused, searching for the others. Seamus sat in a large La-Z-Boy chair, watching soccer on television.

"What was that noise?" asked Declan.

Seamus shrugged. "House is infested with banshees. Removing them is on the to-do list."

"Nice. You hear someone scream, and you can't even get up?"

"That was an *oh no* scream. Not an *I'm dying scream.* I know the difference."

The glass door that led to the back porch slid open, and a group reentered. Making a quick headcount, Charlotte found Mariska missing.

"Check up here. I'll go downstairs," she said, already jogging down the stairs that led to the lowest level.

"Mariska?"

Charlotte felt she was on the right track. The scream had sounded far away and Mariska-esque.

As Charlotte reached the last step, Mariska's answer came in the form of an anguished moan.

The three dogs sat at the far side of the small, lower-level room, their faces glistening, tongues flicking. Their shiny muzzles said *I may have eaten something I shouldn't have.* But their expressions said *I don't know what happened. This woman just went crazy. I'm sure it's nothing we did.*

Mariska stood staring at the dogs, her hands outstretched, aghast. At her feet lay the Thanksgiving turkey, packaging torn open, carcass mangled.

Charlotte's gaze bounced back and forth between the mutilated turkey and the greasy-faced dogs.

Ah.

"What happened?" asked Charlotte, for no other reason than to break the silence. She didn't need to be a detective to piece together *this* puzzle.

"I put the cooler on the table. *On the table*," said Mariska. Her upturned palm gestured toward the cooler as if it were a freshly turned letter on *Wheel of Fortune.*

The cooler now lay on the ground. The table where it had allegedly once perched was too tall for Abby to have leapt on it. Turbo's legs were as long as a human thumb, and Izzy would need a forklift to get off the ground, so they were cleared as suspects.

Charlotte's attention moved to the table's untucked, matching chair.

Ah ha.

"Was that chair pulled out when you got here?" she asked.

Mariska glanced at it. "I guess. I haven't touched anything."

Puzzle solved. Abby was a food Houdini. She'd pushed out the chair, jumped on it, and then continued to the tabletop. Pushing the cooler off the table popped off the lid. Then she, Izzy, and Turbo had an early Thanksgiving.

Abby had once used the same trick at home, though that time, Charlotte had caught her standing on the kitchen table, licking the last of a stick of butter.

"What are we going to do now?" moaned Mariska.

"We'll get another turkey. We have two weeks before Thanksgiving."

"It's not summer. This place is a ghost town. They won't have turkeys as nice as this. And the storm—"

Charlotte patted Mariska on the shoulder. "We'll figure something out. Let me get this." She knelt to tackle the mess.

Mariska sighed, heading for the stairs. "Fine. I'm too heartbroken. It would hurt my knees to kneel down there anyway. I'd probably never get back up." She glared at the dogs, her scowl possibly capable of melting a path through the snow all the way to the nearest turkey store.

The dogs licked their chops, oblivious to her disdain.

Charlotte found a box of trash bags and rolled the turkey into one as the dogs watched.

"You're *bad dogs*. You're lucky you didn't get to the bones—you could have choked to death."

She glanced at her slobbery audience, unable to discern if they were contrite or agitated at the loss of the turkey.

Her money was on the latter.

Charlotte found paper towels and did her best to wipe the dogs' faces. By the time she finished Izzy and Turbo, Abby was already sliding her cheek along an old sofa, cleaning her jowls against the cushions.

"No! Bad!" Charlotte said, lunging to stop her.

Abby ran up the stairs, and Turbo scooted behind her, slowing only long enough to tackle the stairs themselves. Her stubby legs made each stair an individual hurdle.

One, two, jump! One, two, jump!

Izzy labored up last, looking as if she'd like to kill the person who invented stairs.

Charlotte hefted the trash bag over her shoulder like Turkey Santa and followed in the footsteps of the dogs.

Declan waited for her at the top of the stairs.

"I heard," he said.

She handed him the roll of paper towels. "Find my little witch and wipe her mouth, if you would. She's trying to wipe it on the furniture."

"Are they going to be all right?"

Charlotte sighed. "Mariska takes things like this hard at first, but—"

"I meant Abby and the dogs."

"Oh. Yes. They didn't get to the bones, but I wouldn't be shocked if they were sick at some point. That is if Mariska lets them live that long."

Charlotte hauled the turkey into the kitchen.

"What are you doing?" asked Mariska.

"It's still in pretty good shape. I didn't know if you wanted to keep it—"

"We can't cook a turkey the dogs have been *chewing*. Bob, take that from her. It's over twenty pounds."

Charlotte passed the trash-bag-wrapped bird to Bob as if it were a fat baby.

"We can't keep that turkey carcass in here. It'll stink to high heaven," said Darla.

Mariska agreed. "Take it to the can."

Bob scowled and pointed as Abby and Turbo came running into the room, Declan chasing behind them. Izzy had already planted herself for a nap.

"They're the ones that did it. Why do I have to suffer?" asked Bob.

Charlotte held out her hands. "Give it back. I'll take it out to the trash *and* take them with me. They can run around and get their barf out of the way."

Bob passed the turkey to her. "If you insist."

Charlotte spotted a large jacket and a pair of old boots near the back door. She set down the turkey long enough to slip into them and then walked onto the second-story porch, holding open the door for the non-napping dogs. Abby streaked outside and ran down the stairs, Turbo behind her, hopping one step at a time.

Plunk. Plunk. Plunk.

Charlotte remained on the porch a minute longer, resting the mangled turkey on the banister, her face turned to the rising wind. From her perch, she could see the gray, churning sea. It reminded her of a ruined painter's palette—as if a bright turquoise had encroached on a blob of black acrylic and ended up an achromatic splotch of *blah*. The sky was as gloomy as the deep. Only the frothy white breakers scrambling toward the shore gave the scene any punch.

Charlotte cocked her head, considering those incoming streaks of white. The water seemed *closer* than she remembered it being when they arrived.

She shrugged. *It must be high tide.*

Hefting the turkey once more, she headed down the porch stairs. A gust of frigid air flipped away the hood of her jacket and wormed its way into her ears. In the yard, the dogs sniffed and jogged from one spot to the next, unconcerned about her achy ears or the weight of the turkey they'd sampled.

Emboldened by Charlotte's presence, Abby mounted the dunes, streaking toward the beach.

"Stay close!" she screamed at the retreating nub of a beige tail.

Abby looped and returned, as happy to be running in one direction as the other, as long as it meant running through the sprinkling snow. A thin sheet of the icy fluff had collected on the sand.

Charlotte shivered.

This temperature shouldn't even be possible.

Snow was pretty as a novelty, but months of cold wouldn't be something that held any interest for her. The Florida weather had thinned her blood.

Hugging the building beneath the second-story porch, Charlotte clomped along in her oversized boots. Finding no trashcans, she stood, bag in one hand, her other fist balled against her hip.

Where do North Carolina people keep their trashcans?

She heard an angry coughing noise and looked up to see a squirrel balanced on a wire that led to the house. It barked at the dogs and then scampered to the roof. Abby ignored it, jumping in the air to catch flakes while Turbo ripped back and forth through the collecting snow. The light dusting was like a blizzard for the stubby-legged pee wee.

At the end of the yard, past the temporarily insane terrier and rapidly disappearing mini dach, Charlotte spotted a trashcan laying on its side where it had rolled against a wooden-picket dune fence.

There it is.

Tromping to the can, she righted it. It felt heavier than she'd expected. Lifting the lid, she saw a trash bag nestled at the bottom.

The renters before them must have put their final bag inside before leaving.

Leaning in, she gave the loosely-tied top of the half-filled bag a yank, thinking it would be nice to slip the turkey inside of it. It would be added protection toward keeping the smell of the rotting meat from attracting animals.

Old habits born of a much warmer climate.

She tugged, but the bag stuck fast.

What is this? Some kind of joke trash that can't be moved?

She jerked the bag again, only to have the top rip away.

Whoops.

She stood staring at the chunk of plastic in her hand, puzzling at the previous tenant's obstinate trash. She spotted something at the bottom of the bin glistening in the dim sunlight, and her Florida brain made a tremendous leap outside its comfort zone.

Ice.

That's what held the bag in place.

She reasoned that water in the trashcan had frozen to the bag, pinning it to the floor of the bin. Maybe the garbage collectors *had* tried to take it and failed. Her conclusion that the previous renters were lazy, no-good, non-trash-putter-outers might have been premature.

There'd be no moving the bag now, not with the top torn off and no warmth in sight. She dropped the ripped plastic back into the can and was about to drop the turkey on top when something *in* the torn bag caught her eye.

Funny. That looks just like a—

Leaning closer to inspect, the object appeared even *more* like—

No.

She struggled in her borrowed, oversized coat to find her phone. When she did, she turned on the built-in flashlight and shone it into the can.

Yep.

That's a human finger.

CHAPTER SIX

"It can't be *real*," said Carolina, squinting at the finger that sat on a plate in the center of the large kitchen table.

Charlotte had fished a piece of paper from the trash, using it to grab the finger and tote it inside. Abby had followed after her, jumping to sniff the digit, probably hoping to get a taste.

Ghoul dog.

After studying her discovery, Declan and Seamus went outside to sift through the rest of the trash in the leftover bag. Bob and Chuck opted to watch them from the warmth of the house, glasses of bourbon in hand.

"It's probably a leftover Halloween toy," said Mariska.

Chuck wandered over with a fork in his hand and poked the finger with a prong. The skin dimpled and remained that way as he removed the pressure. "It's so *gray*."

"Zombie stuff is pretty hip now. Maybe it's part of a zombie costume," offered Charlotte.

"Maybe you should taste it," suggested Bob.

All eyes turned to him, and he lofted an upturned palm. "What? Tasting it would take the guesswork out of it. Am I wrong?"

"You know what a finger tastes like?" asked Mariska.

He shrugged. "I know what *my* finger tastes like, and it isn't plastic. We could tell if it was a toy or actual meat."

"You're disgusting," said Carolina.

"You know what I can't stop thinking about," said Darla, tilting her head as Chuck poked the finger with his fork a second time. "The next person to rent this place who uses *that* fork to eat off *that* plate."

Carolina grunted. "You people are sickos."

Charlotte chuckled. "I didn't think about that when I grabbed the plate. I had to put it on *something*. Slapping it on the table didn't seem right."

Mariska stood. "All the same, let's agree to keep that plate and fork in a separate place for the remainder of our trip."

"Agreed," chimed the others.

"But you're still going to put it back in the cabinet for the next guy when we leave?" asked Charlotte.

Mariska nodded. "I'm not going to be charged for losing a plate."

A frigid breeze whipped through the house as Declan and Seamus returned from outside.

"Cold out there?" asked Bob. He held up his tumbler of bourbon, and Chuck clinked his own glass against it in a toast.

"It's freezing," said Declan.

Bob finished the little he had left and pointed at the bottle of Woodford Reserve. "Hit me."

"Beat the stuffing out of *me*," said Seamus, grabbing a glass from the cabinet and slapping it on the counter near Chuck's.

Declan rubbed his upper arms and bounced in place. "I didn't even know it could get that cold."

"I had the same thought," said Charlotte.

Carolina rolled her eyes. "Bunch of babies. It's thirty-two degrees out there. That's balmy in Michigan."

None of the Floridians had brought temperature-appropriate clothing. For their foraging expedition, Seamus had claimed Chuck's coat, and Declan had squeezed into Carolina's. His hands were red, dangling from the violet sleeves.

"Didja find anythin'?" asked Darla.

"Nothin' that shouldn't be there," said Seamus, removing Chuck's jacket. He noticed the spare jacket on the line of pegs by the door and looked at Declan. "Why didn't you wear this one?"

Declan scowled. "I didn't see that one."

"Admit it. You just wanted to wear the pretty purple one," said Seamus.

"You got me." Declan hung Carolina's jacket beside the others.

"We should call the police," said Mariska.

Seamus shook his head. "Storm would make getting here difficult. Anyway, if we do, we'll have cops crawling all over the place, keeping us from getting anything done. It can wait."

Carolina's eyes bugged. "It can *wait*? How am I supposed to live in a murder house?"

"In all fairness, the owner of the finger's not necessarily *dead*," said Bob.

"But he's not as good at the piano as he used to be," added Chuck.

Bob raised his glass again. "To pianos."

Seamus and Chuck toasted him. "To pianos."

Carolina huffed. "Bunch of drunks."

Charlotte smiled at Carolina, who always served as a one-woman temperance league. "Don't worry. It'll be fine. For all we know, it's a toy. A disturbingly realistic toy."

"I dunno. It smells kinda funky," said Darla, her nose wrinkling.

Mariska grimaced. "It's getting warm. I'll put it in a

Tupperware."

"Death warmed over," mumbled Darla.

Carolina held up a hand. "I swear, Mariska, don't you *dare* put that finger in the refrigerator with the food."

Mariska opened all the cabinets and, finding no plastic containers, returned to the table with a wad of paper towels and a cut-crystal, covered butter dish. She used the towels as a makeshift glove to roll the finger onto the dish and then covered her prize.

"That's museum quality now," said Declan, admiring the finger-under-glass.

"It's like a little see-thru coffin for it," agreed Darla.

Charlotte moved the butter dish from the table to the counter and pushed it away from the edge.

"Safer over here. Abby has a way of getting on tables," she explained.

Moving to the window, she stared outside as the last of the dim light faded. Two black cats sat on the dunes behind the house, staring up at her, their dark coats speckled with snow.

Declan joined her and followed her gaze.

"Am I seeing two black cats?" he asked.

She nodded. "Yep."

"That's not ominous at all."

"Nah."

Mariska pantomimed brushing her hands free of the severed finger problem, and opened the refrigerator. "Thank you, Carolina, for doing all the shopping early. Thank goodness you did."

Caroline shrugged.

Mariska hung on the door, staring into the refrigerator. "The refrigerator's full of meat. Don't you want it in the freezer?" She opened the freezer door and gasped. "What's *this*?"

"What's what?" asked Carolina.

The freezer was stuffed with packages of meat, leaving barely an inch of open space. The fridge had even more meat piled high.

"You told me to pick up dinners," said Carolina.

Seamus glanced into the freezer and whistled. "Maybe someone *did* chop up the last renters. I think we just found the rest of them."

Mariska scowled. "Carolina, there must be twenty steaks in here."

"Right, eight people, seven days..." Carolina's expression fell. "Oh. You're right. My math is off."

Mariska sniffed. "I would say so—"

"I should have bought more."

"*More*? Carolina, there's nothing but *beef* in here."

"You said to buy *dinners*."

"Who eats meat every day?"

Carolina and Chuck looked at each other.

"Who *doesn't* eat meat every day?" asked Chuck.

"Weirdo hippies, that's who," said Carolina.

Mariska sighed. "The meat in the fridge will go bad before we can eat it and it doesn't all fit in the freezer."

Carolina shook her head like a wet dog. "No, it won't. First, we'll eat it all. Second, I've been rotating the meat in the fridge and freezer once a day. It will last forever."

Charlotte leaned to whisper to Declan. "She learned that trick catering the Donner party."

Declan barked a laugh and quickly sobered when Carolina's glare shot in his direction.

Mariska frowned, and Charlotte watched Carolina's ire rise.

"Oh I'm *sorry*. What do Florida people eat? *Vegetables*?" Carolina spat the last word as if it *tasted* like vegetables.

Mariska huffed. "We don't live on meat *alone*. Does that

mean you didn't buy anything green?"

"I bought vegetables," said Carolina, marching to the cabinet under the sink. She jerked it open and pointed. "Happy?"

Ten-pound bags of potatoes filled the large space.

Mariska gaped. "They're not vegetables. They're *potatoes*."

Charlotte tried to interject. "Well, technically potatoes are veg—"

Mariska barreled on. "Is that all you bought?"

"*No*." Carolina opened the cabinet next to the first to reveal more potatoes.

"So we won't starve, but scurvy is going to be an issue," said Declan under his breath.

Charlotte laughed out loud, and the two sisters turned their heads in tandem to glare at her.

Charlotte tugged on Declan's arm. "Let's go get to work. It's about to get all Polish sisters in here."

CHAPTER SEVEN

It was a little too early for dinner and a little too late for lunch by the time they'd settled down and realized how hungry they were, so the eight of them had steak and potatoes for *linner* as the storm raged outside.

"I don't know whether I want to get to work or take a nap," said Charlotte taking her plate to the sink.

"I'll do the dishes, and you paint," said Mariska, handing her own plate to Bob.

Bob grimaced. By *I'll do the dishes*, Mariska meant *he* would do the dishes. She'd trained him well in that department. She cooked, and he cleaned. There would be no questioning what had been decided long ago.

Darla hopped on the house's ancient computer, tucked in a nook behind the kitchen table. "Look at Brenda," she said, pointing to the screen.

Charlotte peered over Darla's shoulder to see her Facebook timeline. In a photo, their vacation house benefactor, Brenda Scott, sat on a beach, smiling, palm trees serving as a backdrop.

"Where's Phil?" she asked as photo after photo of Brenda rolled by. In the last one, Brenda grinned in front of what looked like an adorable restaurant, a giant macaw parrot perched on her shoulder.

"He's the one taking the photos, I imagine," said Darla. She typed, *Cute! Where's Phil?* in the comments.

"Her vacation looks a little better than ours."

Charlotte moved to the window. The snow had turned to rain as the tropical storm arrived to battle the advancing cold front. It seemed neither of the dying super-storms had the strength to push the other aside. Instead, they spun, locked in battle, and stalled over the Outer Banks of North Carolina.

Perfect timing.

There's nothing left to do but start painting.

Moving from the window, Charlotte noticed a guestbook on the kitchen peninsula. She flipped it to the last entry.

Weather was so-so but had a great time. Kids appreciated the house's collection of board games. Pat & Angie Pinkerton, Seven Valleys, PA.

Charlotte's gaze wandered to the finger laying in its crystal coffin.

Too big to be a kid's finger.

She thought maybe the Pinkerton kids had taken a game of *Mouse Trap* way too seriously.

It wouldn't hurt to do a little snooping.

Pulling her phone from her pocket, Charlotte searched for the Pinkertons of Seven Valleys, Pennsylvania. She found an Angie Pinkerton listed as a PTA contact on a local school website and dialed the number.

"Hello?" said a woman's voice.

"Hi, is this Angie?" asked Charlotte, her mind whirring with possible ways to inquire as to how many fingers Angie's family possessed before and *after* their recent vacation in North Carolina.

There was a pause on the other end of the line before Angie's voice returned, sounding more sour than her initial greeting. "Is this a sales call?"

"No. Sorry. My name is Charlotte. I'm in North Carolina,

staying in the same house you rented last week."

The suspicious tone left Angie's voice. "*Two* weeks ago. Oh no. Did we leave something there? Was it the phone charger? I told them to check all the outlets—"

"No, it's—well, maybe it's worse than that, or nothing at all."

She heard only silence on the line.

"Hello? Angie?"

"What is this?" asked Angie, sounding agitated once more.

Charlotte replayed her last statement in her head and realized how awful it sounded.

"I'm sorry. I'm not trying to scare you. I'm just finding it hard to ask—tell you what—I'm just going to say it. Did any of you lose a finger while you were here?"

Silence.

Charlotte continued for fear of losing her audience. "I know it sounds crazy, but we found a finger. In the trash. It has us a little curious, to say the least."

Angie found her voice again. "You're saying you found a *human* finger in the trash?"

"Yes. In the trash, you, or someone else before us, left behind. Unless it's some kind of prop? Maybe a super-realistic, leftover Halloween thing your kids might have—"

"*My kids don't play around with severed fingers.*" Angie's voice was so icy Charlotte had to assume the temperature had dropped in Pennsylvania as well. She stared at the finger and spoke her observations allowed.

"It's really less *severed* as it is torn or...*chewed* off."

"If this is some kind of sick joke—"

"It's not. I swear."

Charlotte sighed. *Time to wrap it up.*

"I'll let you go. Just to be clear, you're saying your family has all their fingers and toes, right?"

Angie paused. "Wait—is it a finger, or is it a toe?"

"Would it change your answer?"

"*No*. We didn't lose any body parts, and believe me, if we had, I would have been the first to know."

Charlotte thought she heard Angie chuckle. It seemed she'd relaxed, and Charlotte took her at her word. "Okay. I didn't mean to frighten you. There's just no nice way to ask if this finger is yours."

"So—wow. You really found a finger? And you have no idea where it came from?"

"No. Did you notice anything odd while you were here?"

"We saw a horse on the beach."

"I'm thinking odder than that."

"Right. Hm. There were ghost crabs. The kids were herding them into little crab corrals."

"But no knife-wielding maniacs, people with nine fingers, that sort of thing?"

"No, thank goodness."

"Well, I appreciate you hanging in there with me. I'll give you my number in case you think of anything."

"I've got it on the caller ID. I'll ask my husband if he can think of anything. I probably won't ask the kids. I don't want to know if they know where it came from."

It was Charlotte's turn to laugh. "Thank you. I appreciate that."

She disconnected.

"Did you just ask a stranger if they're missing a finger?" asked Mariska.

Charlotte nodded and pointed at the guestbook. "The last people to stay here."

Mariska raised the glasses she wore around her neck and peered at the book.

"You mean the second to last."

"Second?"

"They stayed two weeks ago." She pointed at the date beside the entry.

"Right. The lady I just talked to corrected me on that point. But they're the last entry."

Mariska shrugged. "Not everyone signs the book."

"Especially when they spend their vacation snipping off people's fingers," said Bob from his station at the sink.

"Stop being disgusting and finish those dishes," said Mariska.

Bob frowned. "The sink won't drain."

Charlotte sighed as Mariska and Bob spun into an argument on how to wash dishes in a broken sink.

"I need to find Darla and ask her for Brenda's info. She should be able to tell us who stayed here last." Charlotte said the words to explain her exit but doubted anyone was listening.

She searched for Darla and soon found her in her room. Darla had set out the paint cans and lined up the rollers and brushes across the floor beneath the room's large windows. Windows were good for light *and* for occupying wall space that didn't have to be painted.

"This room is just *paint*, no other fixes," Darla said as Charlotte entered.

"Why are we all painting so late? Won't the fumes knock us out in our sleep?"

"It's green paint. No fumes. Neat, huh? I saw it on TV and asked Carolina to pick up this type. Figured we'd need it. Not like we can spend all our time on the porch here."

Charlotte nodded. "No kidding. Hey, before we get started, do you have Brenda's phone number? I want to ask her who stayed here last week, if anyone."

"She's in Puerto Rico, but I can give her cell a try. She probably won't get back to us right away."

Charlotte frowned. Waiting for information was one of

the worst parts of solving a case. At least this time, she didn't have to sit in a car and stare at a door. Stakeouts were the *absolute* worst.

"Okay. Do I need to change into painting clothes?"

"Yes. I said it doesn't *smell*. It's still *paint*."

Charlotte nodded. "Gotcha. I'll go throw on my sloppy clothes and try and let this go for a bit."

Darla cocked her head. "Let what go? The finger?"

"Yes."

"Why does *that* have you all wound up?"

Charlotte paused on her way out the door. "It's a *finger*. Doesn't it make you a little curious how someone's finger might have ended up in our trash?"

Darla shrugged. "I grew up in Tennessee, hon. Findin' fingers and toes and eyelids layin' around was just another day in the life."

"*Eyelids*?" Charlotte whispered the word, her mind scrambling to imagine a way someone might misplace an eyelid.

Darla stopped stirring her can of paint and straightened. "Hey, darlin', before you go, can you help me push this bed away from the wall?"

Charlotte nodded and moved to the head of the bed. Together, they jerked the heavy oak frame away from the wall, making little progress after four good tugs, complete with grunts.

Charlotte wiped her brow for dramatic flair. "Whew. I think it's far enough away for me to get behind it and use the wall for leverage. Pushing might be easier than pulling. Hold on."

Sucking in her breath, she shimmied between the headboard and the wall. Back against the bed, she wedged her foot against the wall and pushed.

The bed made slow, steady progress across the floor.

Once the frame was a leg's-length away from the wall, Charlotte dropped her foot back to the ground.

Wet.

Something squished beneath her heel, and she shrieked, jumping away from the sensation.

Darla grabbed her chest. "What is it? Spider?"

"Worse. Something *wet* under the bed."

"Snake?"

Charlotte's lip curled, and she took another step back. "Do you think that's possible?"

Darla shrugged and took two steps back.

Keeping her bare feet far from the bed, Charlotte turned on the bedside lamp and slowly squatted, wincing as she prepared for a rare North Carolina Land Eel to leap out at her.

A tattered blob lay on the wood flooring behind the bed. Having never seen a snake that shape before, she crawled closer.

One side of the blob had been squished flat, no doubt by her heel. Overall, the mass had the same gray color and texture as the finger—

Oh no.

CHAPTER EIGHT

Charlotte swallowed and stood to face Darla. "Do you have gloves in here?"

Darla moved to a pile of painting gear and bent to snatch a plastic bag from the heap. "I've got a whole bag of 'em. Need a pair? What did you step on?"

Charlotte held out her hand. "Hard to say at the moment."

Darla tore open the bag and handed Charlotte a pair of blue rubber gloves. Charlotte pulled one on and squatted again to inspect the blob.

The object resembled the finger they'd found in every way except that it wasn't a finger. It had no nail and no bone structure. She poked at it, and it dimpled, before slowly regaining shape, like time-lapse photography of a growing plant. The bumpy texture looked like fat and flesh, though any blood it may have possessed had faded to a sickly gray-brown.

Charlotte pinched the fleshy chunk between her thumb and index finger and pulled it away from the ground. Viscous strings stuck to the floorboards, growing thinner and thinner until they snapped to rejoin the rest of the globule.

"What is *that*?" asked Darla.

Charlotte held the blob aloft for Darla to see. "My guess? A chunk of flesh."

"*Flesh*? Or meat?"

"What's the difference?"

"Flesh is always *people*. Meat is stuff like what we had for—" Darla wrapped her hands over her stomach, the color draining from her face. "Oh, I can't let my mind put those two thoughts together. I might be sick."

Charlotte flipped the chunk and squinted at it. "This side has writing on it."

"Really? What's it say? *If found, please return to body?*"

"Looks like *A-R*, a capital A and R."

"A-R?" Darla gasped. "*Turbo.*"

"Huh? There's no 'A' in Turbo."

"No, Turbo ate the turkey. He's small enough to get under there. He probably barfed a chunk. Probably said *Turkey* or whatever they stamp on turkeys. *Premium gobbler.*"

"*Premium gobbler* doesn't have a A-R in it. Neither does *turkey*, for that matter."

Darla huffed. "*Whatever.*"

Charlotte felt her shoulders relax. "You're right. That totally makes sense."

"You scared the heck out of me. That's probably what that thing downstairs is, too." Darla motioned in the direction of the stairs.

"What thing? The *finger*? We found that in a tied bag of trash. And turkeys don't have fingers or fingernails."

"My grandkids eat chicken fingers every day."

"Very funny."

Darla winked. "Anyway. I'm sure *this* mystery is the turkey."

Charlotte looked at the chunk of flesh clamped between her fingers and tilted her head. "Maybe I'll keep it with the finger, just in case."

Darla turned back to her painting preparations. "Suit

yourself. It's turning into quite a diorama of death down there."

Charlotte jogged the chunk downstairs and slipped it under the crystal lid of the butter dish before returning upstairs to change. As she passed Darla's room on the way to Declan's, Darla called out to her.

"Leave your bags there for now unless they're in Declan's way."

Charlotte stopped, pirouetted, and walked back to Darla's door.

"What's that?"

Darla looked up and blew a chunk of hair out of her eyes. "I said when you get changed, leave your luggage in Declan's room for now. So we don't have to paint around it."

Charlotte hooked her mouth to the side. "Why would I bring my luggage *here*?"

"Because we're bunkmates. Why would you leave your clothes in his room? You don't want to have to knock on his door every time you need to change."

Charlotte scowled. "Who said I was sleeping in here with you?"

Darla put the first stroke of robin's egg blue on the wall. "Declan. He tried to bring your luggage in here, but I sent him away."

Scowling, Charlotte continued to the room she *thought* she was sharing with Declan.

"So you kicked me out?"

Declan crouched on the floor, laying newspaper for painting. He looked up, and upon seeing her expression, his smile fell.

"Uh oh."

"I thought we agreed you wouldn't worry what everyone thought while we were here?"

"Carolina made it clear she was *very* interested to know

more about the sleeping arrangements, and I broke. Sorry."

Charlotte gestured to the colorfully painted bunk beds Declan had pushed into the center of the room. "They're *children's* beds in here. What kind of horn dogs does she think we are?"

Declan shrugged.

Charlotte sighed. "Now I have to share a bed with Darla and Turbo. They both snore like muscle cars." Charlotte put her hands on her hips, surveying Declan's painting preparations. "I don't know if we can get these rooms done today."

"It'll be tight. We spent too much time rummaging around for body parts."

Charlotte perked. "Oh, I almost forgot. Speaking of body parts, I found another."

"You *did*? Another finger?"

"No. Unidentifiable blob. Darla thinks that it's turkey Turbo barfed. I threw it in the butter coffin just in case."

"Ugh." Declan grabbed a brush and handed it to Charlotte. "Ready?"

"Oh no, mister. I came to change for painting, but I'm not doing *your* room."

"*My* room? Oh. I get it. You're helping Darla."

"Yep."

He offered her a lopsided grin. "I guess I deserve that."

She nodded. "You deserve *worse*. I'm going to record Darla and Turbo snoring and play it for you. Then you'll *really* understand what you've done to me."

CHAPTER NINE

Seamus' room was the size of a walk-in closet, so it didn't take him long to paint it the festive pink that had been chosen for him. When he finished, he strolled to the to-do list, which hung pinned to the side of the refrigerator by a pizza delivery magnet.

His plan was to finish *all* his chores on the first day and then take the rest of the vacation off.

The to-do list was printed out on a sheet of white paper in an unnecessarily large font.

DAY ONE:
Everyone paints their own room.

Seamus smiled. *Check!*

DAY TWO:
Paint living areas.

He grimaced. More painting. But he'd heard Mariska complaining about a slow sink. He could tackle that. No one else would.

Chuck and Bob had sucked him into a conversation where he'd felt compelled to brag about being a Jack-of-all-trades. It had been a trap. As soon as the boast left his lips, he'd realized his mistake. The two old men pounced, declaring they had *no* skills at all. In that way, they'd tricked him into taking responsibility for every chore that required any skill. Metaphorically, they'd Tom-Sawyer'd him into painting their fence.

Seamus sighed and hoped for the best. A slow drain could be as easy as pouring some drain cleaner or as hard as dismantling all the pipes.

Darla entered the kitchen and grabbed a Coke from the corner of the fridge they'd declared *meat-free.* She had light blue paint on her nose, cheeks, and hair.

"Done painting?" she asked.

Seamus nodded and tapped the list. "Goin' to knock out this slow drain."

Darla nodded and headed back upstairs. "Brenda said they already tried Draino, so that ain't it."

Seamus hung his head.

It's never easy.

In an attempt to delay crawling beneath the sink, he spent a minute staring through the sliding doors that led to the back porch. The winds had picked up, and the ocean had crept closer to the house than he'd imagined it could. The long beach they'd driven to reach the house had disappeared, replaced by churning water.

They were as stranded as if they were on an island.

He shrugged.

Oh well. I love steak.

Seamus walked across the kitchen to test the drain. Turning on the water, he watched with dismay as the sink filled. Only the occasional bubble rose from the drain to imply a *trickle* might be escaping down the pipe.

So much for hoping it had fixed itself.

He opened the doors under the sink and removed

cleaning products and potatoes to make room for his thick frame. Once the cabinet was clear, he rolled downstairs to the utility room to find the tools he needed. The house's collection of old paint cans, wrenches, hammers, screwdrivers, and other accessories was impressive. The wall had a peg board with the shapes of tools traced on it. Most had tools occupying the spaces, but for what looked like a hacksaw and a pair of pliers.

Luckily, the plumber's wrench *was* in its spot.

Grabbing a plastic store bag he found wadded in the corner of the room, Seamus filled it with the tools he needed and returned to the kitchen to squeeze himself under the sink. Grunting as he worked to wrench apart the pipe, he didn't hear that someone had entered the kitchen until they yelped.

"Ooh!"

The sound made Seamus jump and slam his skull into the underside of the sink.

"Oof!"

He slid out, hand on his head, eyes squinted in pain.

Mariska stood at the edge of the kitchen, her own eyes squinted in empathetic pain, her hand on her head.

"You scared me. I didn't expect to see you there," she said.

"Who did you think I was?"

"I don't know. A burglar?"

He rubbed his head, his voice rising an octave. "What kind of burglar breaks into a house and crawls under the sink?"

"Don't they steal copper pipes?"

Seamus grimaced. She had a point.

There was a clatter as the P-trap fell from the pipe he'd been working on and dropped to the bottom of the cabinet.

Seamus glanced at the P-trap, and a flash of yellow caught his eye. Tucked in a clump of greasy mess, bright gold gleamed against the muck that had dislodged from the pipe when it fell.

Gold!

He leaned back into the cabinet, expecting to find a ring or other piece of jewelry.

Finders, keepers, losers—

His grin dropped as fast as it had appeared. He glanced at Mariska to see if she'd noticed what he'd pulled from the pipe.

She was busy reading the to-do list.

Shimmying from the cabinet, he stood, closing the cabinet doors behind him.

"So, can I help you with anything?" he asked Mariska.

Mariska dismissed him with a wave. "Oh, don't let me stop you. I just wanted a bottle of water." She opened the refrigerator and studied its contents for some time.

"Let me guess. Carolina didn't buy water?"

"No. Guess it's cola for me," Mariska grabbed a soda and, with a little wave, disappeared in the direction of the stairs.

Seamus peered around the corner to watch her mount the stairs and then scurried back to the sink and flung open the door. Fumbling for a flashlight, he shined it on the clump of things that had tumbled out of the P-trap.

He'd seen gold, but it wasn't jewelry. What he'd thought was treasure turned out to be a tooth filling, still attached to the tooth.

And a good chunk of gum tissue.

Pulling his penknife from his pocket, Seamus poked through the glob of hair and grease. The disgusting mess inspired unwelcomed flashbacks of his time in Miami, where he'd bartered part of his rent performing handyman tasks. He'd needed spare cash often enough that he'd become the unofficial super of his building. The things he'd pulled from drains over the years ranged from disgusting to repulsive, but he'd never found a *tooth*.

The amount of hair and grease in the drain, in combination with the tooth...

Seamus pushed the tooth aside and scooped the rest of the gunk into the bag he'd used as a makeshift toolbox. He balled it up and threw it in the back of a drawer that held nothing but obscure kitchen utensils. He didn't want to lose what could be valuable evidence, but he also didn't want anyone bumping into the gunk.

He rooted through the other drawers until he found a sandwich bag and then returned his attention to the tooth beneath the sink.

Careful to avoid the gum tissue, he plucked the molar from the floor of the cabinet and dropped it in the sandwich bag before carrying it upstairs to Declan's room.

"Hey."

In mid-paint stroke, Declan turned.

"Hey. Done your room?"

"A while now. It's tiny."

"I thought you were being magnanimous taking the small room, but you knew you'd have to paint it. I should have known there was a method to your madness."

Seamus flashed him a quick smile to let him know his deduction was correct. "Where's Charlotte?"

"Helping Darla."

"What's up?" said a voice behind Seamus. Charlotte had appeared as if invoked. "My ears were burning."

Seamus checked down the hall and ushered her into Declan's room. She entered, and he shut the door behind her.

"Ooh, this is very mysterious," she said.

He raised his hand with the bag pinched between his thumb and forefinger.

Standing several feet away, Declan and Charlotte's necks both telescoped toward the bag.

"What's that?" asked Declan.

Charlotte retracted her head with a gasp. "A *tooth*. Where

did you find it?"

"In the sink trap."

She leaned closer. "Is that *gum* attached to it?"

Seamus nodded. "Whoever lost this one didn't lose it easily."

"Oh, I see now," muttered Declan. He rested his roller in the paint tray and moved in to inspect Seamus' trophy. "That is *gross*."

Charlotte shook her head. "A finger, a hunk of meat, a tooth..."

Seamus scowled. "A hunk of meat?"

"I found a chunk of flesh under the bed in Darla's—" She shot Declan a scowl. "I mean in *my* room."

"Human?" asked Seamus.

"Darla thinks it's a hunk of turkey Turbo barfed up, but I don't know. I put it with the finger. Did you find anything else?"

Seamus pushed the bag into his pocket. "Hair, fat, grease. The usual. Except when you've already found larger chunks of people, you have to wonder if someone didn't dismember a body in the sink."

Charlotte's eyes grew wide. "Yikes. It *might* be time to call the police."

Seamus shook his head. "Tide's eaten the beach. We're stuck here, and no one is coming in. Even if you raise someone on the phone, they can't get here until the water recedes."

Declan rubbed his face with his hand. "So it's official. We *are* stuck in a murder house." He lowered his hand, his face now smeared with paint.

Seamus smiled at Charlotte. "Life still has its precious moments."

She giggled.

Declan scowled, looking from one of them to the other. "What?"

CHAPTER TEN

They managed to make it to dark without finding more people-chunks.

Charlotte walked into her newly assigned bedroom after brushing her teeth, her mind still searching for a logical excuse for what they'd found. Things were either very coincidental—an unbelievably realistic prank finger, a hunk of turkey, and an accident that resulted in the loss of a tooth—or things were horrific; someone had chopped a victim into bits and failed to account for all the parts.

The sight of her bed raised more concerns.

First:

Will a killer be lurking nearby as we sleep tonight?

She shivered at the thought of it.

And second:

Why is Darla on my side of the bed?

She tapped Darla's toe. "You took my side of the bed. You said you liked the right side."

Darla dropped her book into her lap. "My side was taken."

At the sound of Darla's voice, Charlotte heard the thump of a dog's tail. The blankets beside Darla bobbed up and down in time with the beat. Moving to that side of the bed, Charlotte pulled back the sheets to reveal Turbo happily staring up at her, tail still thrumming as he awaited the verdict on whether or not he'd be asked to move.

Charlotte sighed. *How can I ask those eyes to move?*

"I couldn't even take a quick nap today—dang dogs seem obsessed with this room. Hit the light. I'm done reading," said Darla, setting the book on the bedside table.

Charlotte hit the switch and felt her way back to the bed, gently nudging Turbo until she found space to lie down. A moment later, Abby jumped into the bed and flopped at her feet, shoving against her legs with all her weight. Charlotte twisted to snake her body between the two dogs. It wouldn't be the first time she slept awkwardly wrapped around dogs that she couldn't bear to kick out of bed.

Outside, the storm raged, the wind howling.

Between the sound of the rain beating against her window and her whirring mind, Charlotte was sure she'd never fall asleep.

Too much to think about...too much...

She awoke with a start.

Charlotte sat up in bed and glanced at the glowing red digits on the bedside table clock. It was 6:53 a.m. At home, she would have been awake for hours, but they'd stayed up late painting. Guess she fell asleep after all.

"What was that?" mumbled Darla.

Charlotte tried to piece together what had woken her. She didn't have to think for long.

The dogs were barking.

She heard the sound of paws on the stairs, and Abby appeared. Turbo joined a moment later, both of them panting excitedly. Bringing up the rear, Izzy grunted her way into the room, her enormous ears swiveling like satellite dishes.

Darla sat up. "Is that the dogs? I swear, Turbo *never* barks, and now that's twice in as many days."

"Abby must be a bad influence."

Charlotte rose, happy she'd had the foresight to sleep in

her sweatpants and a tee. Outside, she could hear the storm still howling.

Charlotte shuffled to the dogs and scratched Abby's chin.

"What's up, girl?"

The early morning light glowed through their window, and she noticed something white on the floor beside the dogs. She flicked on the light.

The stairs were littered with white paw prints.

Paint.

"They ran through paint somewhere. There are paw prints *everywhere*." The break in Charlotte's voice conveyed the weight of the hours of cleaning it would take to fix the mess, *if* fixing was even possible. There were no carpets in the house, but there were rugs and furniture. Her shoulders slumped at the thought of the mess she couldn't yet see.

Darla clambered out of bed and stood in her nightgown, jaw hanging as she stared at the painted paw prints, both big and small. Somehow, at least two of the dogs had run through the paint.

"Oh no," she moaned.

Darla snatched Turbo into her arms and marched her to the bathroom. Charlotte grabbed the other two by the collar and dragged them after her. Both dogs sensed something was up and planted their feet, but on the polished wood floors, they slid toward their fate.

Charlotte and Darla rinsed their paws in the bathtub and locked the cranky dogs in the tiled room.

It was time to find the epicenter of the disaster.

They found Declan and Seamus staring at them from the bottom of the stairs.

"There are paw prints *everywhere*," said Declan.

"No kidding," said Charlotte, rolling her eyes.

"I see you knew that."

"We just finished cleaning the little monsters' paws," said

Darla.

Seamus rubbed his head and shuffled back upstairs toward his room. "You seem to have things well in hand."

"I found some rags under the sink," said Darla, heading down.

"I'll help," said Declan, taking one.

"Darla, go back to bed. I've got this," said Charlotte.

Darla clucked her tongue. "Oh honey, this is a disaster."

"I'll get to it before it dries. It's no problem. You can't be crawling around on your hands and knees."

Darla made some attempt to argue before heading back upstairs. "I might need another half an hour."

Rag in hand, Charlotte wiped backward down the stairs from her bedroom. Declan started ahead of her, and they skipped over each other's progress until they had worked their way two stories down to the scene of the crime—the lower-level utility room.

A tray of paint sat against the far wall.

"Who painted this room?" asked Charlotte.

"I think that was Bob. He and Mariska had a difference of opinion on how to paint their room, so he took this one."

Charlotte scowled at the nexus of the mess. The shallow tray of white paint had been flipped, and a small pool of paint bled from underneath it. A riot of paw prints led in every direction.

"Look at these..." she said, squatting next to a small set of prints.

"Turbo?"

"No. They aren't dog prints. The toes seem kind of long— maybe they're smeared? Maybe cat prints?"

"What are you, Davey Crocket?"

She chuckled. "Remember? I went through a phase in grade school where I was fascinated with animal tracks."

Declan nodded. "That seems totally normal."

Tracing the tracks, she followed the cat prints to a corner behind the water heater.

"There's a hole in the wall back here," she said, trying to get a better view.

"So the local cats come in and out at will?"

"Looks like—"

Declan cut her short. "Charlotte—"

She pulled her head out from behind the water heater to find Declan pointing to a different corner of the room.

Following his gesture, she saw something on the ground where he pointed.

She moved to it.

"Is that...?"

Declan nodded. "I can't imagine what else it could be."

A shiver ran down Charlotte's back. "That's not from a turkey."

She wasn't looking at something that had come from *any* kind of bird.

She was looking at half a human ear.

There was a loud *boom!* and the lights went out, plunging them into darkness.

CHAPTER ELEVEN

Charlotte and Declan both yelped and grabbed for each other.

"Are we in a dark room with a chewed *ear*?" whispered Charlotte.

She felt Declan's grip on her arm tighten. "I'd say *stranger things have happened*, but I don't think they have."

The low rumble of a distant engine reached their ears.

"Generator?" asked Declan.

She nodded, though she knew he couldn't see. "Clearly, not *our* generator."

"Hello?" said a voice at the top of the stairs.

Charlotte turned her head toward the sound. "Mariska?"

"Did the lights go out down there?"

Charlotte and Declan shuffled toward the stairs, holding hands, but each with the opposite hand stretched in front to keep from smacking into walls. Charlotte had never wished she wasn't barefoot so much in her life.

"It's black down here," Charlotte shouted up the stairs, less to convey the obvious facts of their situation and more to confirm that someone within earshot could call for help when the ear-munching monster grabbed them.

"I was just starting the coffee, and everything went dark. What are you doing down there?" asked Mariska as the couple felt their way up the stairs. Charlotte felt her blood pressure tick a point down upon hearing her voice.

"Bob left a paint tray down here. A cat got in the house, and the dogs chased it through the paint."

"Snitch," said Bob's voice somewhere behind Mariska.

"Did you say a cat?" asked Mariska.

They reached the top of the stairs. The storm clouds weren't allowing much early morning sunlight to reach the windows, but at least they could see.

"There's a hole in the wall down there, behind the water heater," said Charlotte.

"Among other things," muttered Declan. Charlotte shot him a look, hoping to convey that she wanted to keep the ear between them a little longer. He pressed his lips shut.

Charlotte continued rambling, hoping Mariska wouldn't inquire what Declan meant. "That whole place down there is less of a *room* and more of an *enclosure*. The walls are flimsy. I think it's supposed to be storm surge space, but they've turned it into utility space."

"They have a generator next door," said Bob, standing at the side window, peering at their neighbors.

Charlotte nodded. "We heard it kick on."

Mariska returned to the kitchen. "I think I might have made a cup or two before we lost power."

"It's all yours," said Charlotte. She'd seen Mariska without her morning coffee.

Charlotte pulled a chair from the kitchen table and sat. Elbows propped, she dropped her head in her hands. She felt exhausted and now remembered waking on and off throughout the night as either Abby or Turbo stretched to make more room for themselves. For such a tiny dog, Turbo knew how to make his presence known. Darla's snoring hadn't helped, and Turbo had joined in, serving as a tiny echo of his mother's mighty snorts.

Carolina thumped down the stairs in a plaid nightgown

trimmed with white ruffles that covered more flesh than a Victorian mourning gown.

"What are you wearing? A lumberjack's muumuu?" asked Charlotte.

Carolina scowled and playfully shook a small balled fist at her. "Is the electricity out?"

"It is," said Mariska.

Carolina raised her hands. "The *meat*. No one opens the fridge. Don't let out the cold."

Charlotte looked over at Mariska, who had frozen in place, creamer in hand, refrigerator cracked open. She eased the door shut.

"They have a generator next door. Maybe we can ask to store some of the meat over there," said Charlotte, drawing away Carolina's attention while Mariska sneaked the cream back into the fridge.

Declan sat beside her and whispered a single word. "Ear?"

She bit her lip and shook her head. "Let's wait."

She stared out the window at the storm. The gray weather was getting her down. It rained nearly every day in Florida, but it was also sunny nearly every day. And back in Florida, she didn't have a human ear downstairs waiting for her to collect.

While the others gathered in the kitchen to toast bread and cook eggs on the gas stove, Charlotte grabbed a plastic zip-seal bag and sneaked upstairs. She grabbed her phone to use as a flashlight and was about to leave the room when she spotted Darla's tweezers sitting beside a makeup bag. She snatched them and slipped back downstairs to the utility room. Using the tweezers, she grabbed the ear, studied it beneath the phone's flashlight for as long as she could without gagging, and then dropped it into the bag.

"So this is where it started."

Charlotte jumped at the sound of the voice and fumbled

with the tweezers. They dropped to the ground with a tinny clatter.

Darla stood at the bottom of the stairs with a ball of clothing in her arms. Her gaze dropped to the tweezers on the ground. "Are those *my* tweezers?"

"Hm?" Charlotte stared at her phone, where it sat propped on the washer. She'd set up the flashlight to illuminate the room. Without it, Darla wouldn't be able to see a thing.

Would it be suspicious if I reached out and slapped my phone to the ground?

"What were you doing with my tweezers? What's behind your back?" asked Darla.

Charlotte kept the ear behind her back and pointed to the spilled paint with the other.

"I'm cleaning."

"In the dark?"

"I didn't want it to dry."

Darla sat the clothes on top of the washer and stooped to retrieve the tweezers.

"You haven't been scraping paint with my tweezers, have you? You'll ruin them."

"No. I wouldn't do that."

Darla put her hands on her hips and arched an eyebrow. "Charlotte, you know I *know* when you're up to something. What do you have behind your back?"

Charlotte crumpled the bag until she felt the ear inside of it. Her fingers recoiled from the squishy object, but not before her expression had registered her disgust.

Darla's scowl deepened.

"Fine." Charlotte revealed the bag, holding it aloft for Darla to inspect it.

Darla moved to keep from blocking the flashlight and peered at the bag. After a moment, her eyes popped wide. "Is that an *ear*?" she screeched.

Charlotte nodded.

"Turkeys don't have *ears*."

"Not last I checked."

"You found that *here*?" Darla shimmied back, scanning the floor as if she'd just realized she stood on hot coals.

"Right where you're standing."

Darla mounted the lowest step, clinging to the banister railing with her fingers curled like an eagle's talons.

"Where's the rest of him?" she asked.

"Not here. Though I suppose his finger is upstairs," said Charlotte.

"We were down here before. How did we miss an *ear* laying on the floor?"

"See these tracks? They're not the dogs'. I think a cat sneaked in and brought us a trophy."

"Where would a cat get an ear?"

"That is the question, isn't it? Maybe it was in the trash with the finger originally. Not that that explains much."

Darla looked up the stairs. "Do the others know?"

"No. The electricity went out two seconds after Declan, and I spotted it. I thought it would be creepy to tell everyone about it in the dark."

Darla pursed her lips and sighed through her nose. "I'm starting to question if that other chunk you found in our room is from the turkey."

"You and me both."

Darla climbed a few steps and then stopped. "*Now* can we take these bits of John Doe to the police?"

"No. The beach is swamped even at low tide. We're stuck."

Darla huffed and continued up the stairs. Two steps later, she stopped again.

"You used my tweezers to pick up that ear, didn't you?"

Charlotte squinted her eyes. "No?"

Darla shuddered. "This is starting to feel a little like a dang horror movie."

Charlotte nodded and followed. "Little bit."

CHAPTER TWELVE

Charlotte caught up to Darla and asked her to keep news of the ear to herself a little while longer.

"I'd like to have some idea what's going on before we scare everyone," she explained.

Darla grimaced. "I'll do my best, darlin', but something like *we found an ear* is likely to fly out of my mouth at some point."

"Understood."

Charlotte hid the ear in her room and sat on the bed, contemplating her next move. Someone had to have seen *something*. Surely someone couldn't arrive with a person, kill them, chop them into bits, throw them in the bin and then leave without anyone noticing?

Unfortunately, they hadn't yet identified the last people to stay in the house, and most of the houses nearby were rental units—

She straightened.

The nursing home wasn't.

She needed to talk to the people of the Elder Care-o-lina.

Invigorated by her new mission, Charlotte trotted back downstairs, slid into shoes, and donned the jacket they'd inherited with the house before slipping out the door.

Bounding down the porch stairs, she hit the bottom landing and stopped. The back yard had turned into a mud pit. Swirling eddies of brown water danced where once there had been land.

She stepped into the mire and slowed her pace in order to keep her footing and not sacrifice a boot to the sucking slop. Creeping past the neighbor's roaring generator, she braced herself against the driving rain as she rounded the corner of the Elder Care-o-lina. She clomped up the nursing home's front stairs, basking in the light streaming through the glass panels on either side of their front door.

Electric lights. Ah, I remember those.

As the wind bit through her jacket, she realized it would soon grow cold in their electricity-free house. *Cold* for any average person—*freezing* for a mob of Floridians.

She realized that in addition to probing for information about fingers and ears, she needed to find a home for the seventeen dismembered cows huddled in their melting freezer.

Even if the neighbors were murderers, they might have freezer space. No point in alienating them too quickly in case the group needed a warm place to hole up and wait out the storm. If polled, she guessed sixty percent of Floridians would prefer living with killers over temperatures below forty.

Charlotte knocked, and a man she guessed to be in his early sixties answered. He was tall and pudgy, with a balding pate and shy manner.

"Hello. Last thing I expected was a knock on the door. You poor thing. Come in," he said, ushering her inside.

She entered and held out a hand, water puddling at her feet. "Thank you. I'm Charlotte. We're staying next door."

"Nice to meet you, Charlotte. I'm Emmitt. I saw you drive in."

Charlotte laughed. "I imagine you couldn't miss us."

They shook hands, and Charlotte winced as the motion rattled more water to the floor. "I'm making a mess of your foyer."

"Oh, don't worry about it. Take off your coat, and I'll hang it here."

She did, and he secured it to a peg on the wall.

Charlotte looked around the large open living area. It mirrored their own vacation house, except that the walls were painted an aggressive shade of orange. She heard a clatter and a door in the foyer that she'd assumed to be a closet opened. A middle-aged woman in a nurse's uniform walked out, pushing a man in a wheelchair.

She tilted to get a better view and confirmed that the "closet" was, in fact, an elevator.

The nurse's face betrayed her surprise at finding a guest in the foyer.

"You're the ones with the crazy snake bus," she said.

Charlotte nodded. "Guilty as charged."

"Julie, this is Charlotte. Julie is our full-time registered nurse," said Emmitt.

Charlotte stepped out of her boots and moved forward to shake Julie's hand. She'd planned to continue her greeting to the frail man in the wheelchair, but he remained unmoving, seemingly unaware of her presence.

"That's Mr. Remy," added Emmitt.

"He's not really with us anymore," whispered the nurse.

Charlotte nodded and counted the old man's fingers and ears as nonchalantly as she could.

He possessed the usual number.

I suppose that would have been too easy.

An orange tabby cat strolled through the room, never offering Charlotte a moment's consideration.

"You have a cat," she said.

"Three, actually. That's Sherbet, and his buddies, the twins, are somewhere around here."

"The twins are black?" asked Charlotte.

Emmitt's brows knit. "Yes. How did you know?"

"We saw them outside."

He shook his head. "No. They're indoor cats."

Charlotte opened her mouth to disagree and then stopped. Apparently, cats did a lot of things people didn't know about.

She considered asking Emmitt if she could check all the cats' paws for paint but decided against it. Odds were strong that at least one of the cats was their mystery guest, and insisting she *prove* it would make it seem as if she'd only come to complain about the cat's visit.

If somehow they were involved, she didn't want to warn them about finding the ear and give them the opportunity to move a body. It could be that the body was nearby, and the cats were using it as a twenty-four-hour buffet.

She also had to stay true to her prime directive: *Don't alienate the people with a generator.*

She turned her attention back to Emmitt. "It's nice you have a generator. But I guess you *have* to have a generator with patients here."

"Residents, not *patients*," said a shrill voice. A red-headed woman wearing a turquoise track suit swept into the room. Julie had resumed her stroll with Mr. Remy and found herself blocking the approaching woman as the redhead whipped around the corner and attempted to make her grand entrance. The woman scowled at the nurse, shifting to continue her path toward Charlotte. Her frown once again morphed into a beaming smile, her arms outstretched in greeting.

"I'm Dinah. And you are?" She placed a hand on each of Charlotte's shoulders.

"Charlotte. I'm with the group next door."

The woman's hands slid down Charlotte's arms, and she enveloped the right hand with both her own. Charlotte guessed Dinah to be in her late sixties or early seventies. Her ruby hair sat piled high on her head, wavy tendrils spilling left and right from the haystack.

"I'm one of the residents," said Dinah, though she didn't seem to need any sort of assistance.

"She's more of a mascot," said Emmitt with a little smile.

Dinah slapped his arm playfully. "Oh, that makes me sound like some sort of pet. Stop that." She turned to Charlotte. "I enrolled my mother here, and I loved it so much that I moved in a little early. It's like living in a five-star beachside hotel. Why wouldn't I move in?"

"And she's a great help with the other residents," added Emmitt.

"That's wonderful that you can stay so close to your mother," said Charlotte.

Dinah shook her head. "Oh no, Momma's dead, dear. A year ago."

"Oh. I'm sorry."

"No way for you to know. Don't worry yourself."

"So, Charlotte, how can we help you?" asked Emmitt.

Charlotte looked at him as she silently ran through the various reasons she'd come, searching for the most innocuous one to share. "Sorry. I almost forgot why I came. It's your generator."

"Is it too noisy?"

"Oh no, nothing like that. It's just I don't know how long the electricity will be out, and we've got a *lot* of meat, er, *food,* in the freezer. I thought I'd swing by, say *hi*, see how you're all getting along in the storm and ask if you had some space in your fridge, should push come to shove."

"Sure. We have a box freezer downstairs, and we can always make room for a couple of pounds of hamburger," said

Emmitt.

Couple of pounds. Riiight...

"Oh, no, that freezer is on the fritz, remember?" said Dinah, touching Emmitt's arm.

Emmitt scowled for a moment before his expression relaxed. "Oh, you're right. Thank you for reminding me. Well, we can always fit food in the kitchen freezer. How much could it be?"

Charlotte smiled. *You have no idea.*

"Would you like the tour?" asked Dinah. She seemed annoyed that the conversation had wandered to such mundane topics as meat temperatures.

"Sure, that would be great."

"What else is there to do on a day like today?" Dinah grinned and slapped Charlotte's shoulder before raising her own arms to the sky. "This is the foyer," she said, pronouncing it *foy-aye* before twirling toward the kitchen.

"This the kitchen, obviously, and our TV-watching room is there, of course. It's all very similar to your place."

"You're familiar with our place?"

"Am I...oh, not *really*, but all the houses along here are the same, more or less."

"Do you know Phil and Brenda?"

"Who?"

"Phil and Brenda Scott. It's their house. We're helping them fix it up a bit in return for a holiday vacation."

"Oh, no. I haven't had the pleasure. I think James used to do handiwork for them, though." Her gaze shot in Emmitt's direction as if she'd said something she shouldn't have and then barreled on before Charlotte could inquire who James was.

"We've made friends with various groups of renters over the years, but I'm not familiar with the owners there," she said.

"Do you know who was there last week? Before us?"

Dinah thought for a moment and then shook her head. "I can't remember. Emmitt? Did you see who was there last week?"

He shrugged. "Like you said, James would know, but..." Emmitt sniffed and looked away, shaking his head.

Dinah put a hand on Charlotte's arm. "Anyway, the houses are very similar."

"You have an elevator. That's nice," said Charlotte.

"Oh it is. Absolutely a necessity for us, of course. Let's take that now."

Dinah opened the door and slid back the grate with a quick jerk of her arm. Charlotte followed her to the snug box, and she yanked the grate shut again before Emmitt could join them.

"No need to come, Emmitt. We'll see you when we get back."

Emmitt nodded and wandered off.

The elevator moved slowly, but it didn't have far to go. On the second floor, Dinah opened the grate, and they walked into a hallway lined with pictures. In one photo, a dark-haired middle-aged man wearing a Clemson college t-shirt stood with his arm around Dinah and an older woman.

"That's Momma," said Dinah.

"Who's that?" asked Charlotte, pointing to the man.

She scowled. "That's James. He's no longer with us."

"Oh. Sorry again."

"Not dead, dear. *Left*. Not a good fit."

The next picture was of an elderly gentleman in an old-fashioned army uniform standing on the beach.

"Doesn't he look smart," said Charlotte.

"Hm. Mr. Marino. Veteran's Day. Most of the men here are veterans. Never let you forget it, either. Even on the beach."

She pointed to a photo of the same elderly gentleman

sitting in a beach chair, a large Army tattoo on his chest. She rolled her eyes. "They let you know even without their uniforms. Let me show you the rooms."

As Dinah tugged her down the hall, Charlotte tried to catch glimpses of the other photos. They were mostly group shots of people on the beach or sitting on the porch, Emmitt and Dinah always nearby.

They passed an empty room, sparse but for a hospital bed.

"That's Mr. Remy's spot. Now that he's catatonic, he doesn't keep up with his decorating, and he has no family."

Charlotte pointed to a medal pinned to the lampshade beside the bed. "Mr. Remy's a veteran?"

Dinah nodded and moved down the hall to tap lightly on a closed door. "This one is Mr. Hanson. He doesn't get out of bed as much as he used to. Marine corps."

Dinah flung open the door to what appeared to be the master bedroom, the massive windows offering an expansive view of the churning seas. The color palette and decorations implied a woman occupied this room.

"This is my room," said Dinah, beaming with what looked like pride.

"You have the master? Lucky you," said Charlotte.

"Oh I *insisted*. I couldn't move into Momma's old room. That would be absolutely *morbid*. And anyway, what does Emmitt need with the space now that he's alone?"

"Alone?" Charlotte repeated the word before she could stop herself.

Dinah looked at her and raised her eyebrows. "Hm?"

"Oh, sorry, you said now that he's *alone*. It's none of my business—"

"Did I? I just meant because he *is* alone. He doesn't need a big room as a single man."

"Right."

Dinah brushed by her. "Over there is Emmitt's room and Grace's place. Grace was here when momma arrived. She's been here the longest."

A curly white head of hair poked from Grace's opened door.

"Don't mind us, Grace. I'm just giving our neighbor here the tour."

"Are you the police?" asked Grace, her gaze locked on Charlotte.

Dinah rolled her eyes. "Gracey, I've told you a million times. *Murder She Wrote* is on television. It isn't *real*."

Grace nodded and withdrew.

Dinah pulled Charlotte close, her voice dropping to a conspiratorial whisper. "Her kids bought her the complete *Murder She Wrote* collection on DVD, and now she thinks she's *in* them. She thinks I'm Angela Lansbury because of my hair."

Dinah tapped Charlotte's arm as a signal to follow and headed down the stairs. "I like to walk *down* the stairs. It's not as hard as *up* and makes me feel like I've exercised."

Emmitt wandered into the *foy-aye* as they descended.

"Get the nickel tour?" he asked.

"I did. Very nice place you have. It's yours?"

He nodded, his expression growing glum. "James and I started it ten years ago."

Charlotte looked at Dinah, who shook her head, her lips pursed. She pulled Charlotte's coat from the peg and thrust it at her.

Charlotte took the coat and looked back at Emmitt, whose attention had wandered to the floor.

"Thank you for the tour. I'll—" There was a *pop!* and the room grew brighter. The roar of the generator stopped.

Charlotte smiled. "How about that. Power's back. Guess I won't need to bother you with our fridge problems after all."

"No bother," said Dinah, opening the door.

With a final wave, Charlotte crouched and plunged back into the storm.

CHAPTER THIRTEEN

"There you are. We were about to send out a search party," said Declan as Charlotte reentered the rental. He was standing on a ladder in the living room, roller in hand, while Chuck painted the lower half of the room.

"I went next door to see if they had fridge space for our butcher shop."

"I heard that," said Carolina, as she rotated the meat from the freezer to the refrigerator.

"I think you were trying to get out of painting the living room," said Declan.

Charlotte grinned. "Maybe."

"I think she was snooping," said Seamus, descending the stairs. "Any luck?"

Charlotte sighed. "Something weird is going on over there, but they had all their fingers and ears."

"Why wouldn't they have ears?" asked Carolina.

Charlotte slapped her hand over her mouth. Her eyes darted to Declan, who pointed at her.

"What's weird next door?" asked Seamus, unfazed by the mention of ears. Charlotte guessed Declan had told him about their discovery, and he was helping her blow past Carolina's inquiry.

Spurred by his question, she ignored Carolina and continued. "They're running an assisted living home for the elderly. One of the residents, Dinah, has more energy than I do, and she steamrolls over the owner, a big, doofy fellow named Emmitt. There's a lady who thinks she's in an episode of *Murder She Wrote*, catatonic Mr. Remy, a nurse, and a missing man named James who has me curious."

Seamus thrust his hands in his pockets. "Oh? Do tell."

"He's apparently one of the original owners. He started the place with Emmett, but he's gone now. Dinah said he *wasn't a good fit*."

"Maybe Emmitt bought him out, and Dinah called it *fired*. Did you talk to Emmitt about it?"

"No. There's really no logical reason why I should be interested in his ex-partner's whereabouts. And, when he first mentioned James, he looked upset. Oh, and he implied James was over *here*."

"Now? Hiding under the floorboards?" asked Seamus.

"No. In the *past*."

"Why?" asked Declan, climbing a ladder in the main room with a paint roller.

"I think he was helping Brenda and Phil with handyman things."

Seamus cocked an eyebrow. "Well, he wasn't very good if he was here."

"I guess not..." said Charlotte, her voice trailing as she started thinking about her conversations at the Elder Care-o-lina.

"*You're* thinking we've got James' finger in the kitchen, aren't you?" asked Seamus.

Charlotte nodded. "Makes sense, right? But I couldn't ask them if by *left* they really meant *dismembered*. That would have been odd."

"You people have issues," muttered Carolina.

Seamus slowly scratched his chin as if pondering all her news. "Hm. We're on the same page..."

"Yeah, both avoiding painting," grumbled Declan from his perch on the ladder as he strained to reach a spot above one of the large windows.

Darla moved to the computer nook to check her Facebook page.

"Have you heard anything from Brenda?" asked Charlotte, drying her rain-soaked hair with a dish towel.

"That's what I'm checking now," said Darla as she scrolled through Brenda's timeline. Her friend had posted even more photos of fun in the sun in Puerto Rico. Smiling Brenda with a piña colada, a shot of Brenda and Phil on the beach, Brenda feeding a banana to an iguana.

Bob entered and stopped to peer over Darla's shoulder. "I didn't know Phil was a marine," he said.

On his tan chest, Phil had a Marine logo tattoo perched above a Betty Boop-style girl in a grass skirt doing the hula. It reminded Charlotte of Mr. Marino's photo over at the Elder Care-o-lina.

Mariska stopped to investigate the pictures as well. "I'm glad you never got one of those tattoos."

Bob shrugged. "I'm too handsome to scribble on. It would be like spraying graffiti on the statue of David."

Mariska snickered.

It was clear to Charlotte that Brenda hadn't been spending as much time in the sun. Her white skin glowed compared to Phil's.

Charlotte sighed. "I'll be as pale as Brenda by the time we get back to Florida."

"Did Brenda get back to you about who rented the house last week?" asked Seamus.

Darla shook her head. "Not in my email. I'll try to

message her through Facebook since she seems to be checking in there."

"Ask her if she can think of anything suspicious at all," added Charlotte.

Declan looked down from his perch on the ladder. "Listen to you two. You detective types don't know how to have a vacation, do you?"

Seamus raised his eyebrows. "Right. Look at you up there *painting*. You're a one-man party."

Declan grimaced. "Good point."

Charlotte sat on a stool in front of the peninsula that separated the kitchen from the large living room. "We're not being crazy. It's not like we found a single blood drop and started screaming murder. We found a finger and a fleshy blob—"

"And an ear," said Darla from the computer nook.

"An *ear*?" chimed Mariska, Carolina, Chuck, and Bob like the world's worst barbershop quartet.

Darla looked at Charlotte, her eyes wide. "Whoops. I warned you."

"In all fairness, I slipped first," said Charlotte.

"Where did you find an ear? Where did you put it?" asked Mariska, and lifting the butter dish cover, she snarled her lip and closed it again. "We might want to put this in the freezer. It's getting a little ripe."

"We couldn't fit another *hair* in that freezer," said Bob.

"I want to know more about this ear," said Mariska.

Charlotte sighed. The jig was up. "I found it on the floor downstairs. There's a hole in the wall, and I think the neighbors' cats are using it to get in. I think they brought it with them. It's up in my room. "

"In *our* room?" asked Darla.

"It's in a bag."

"I am not sleeping with an *ear* in the room, bagged or not.

Put it down here with the other people-parts."

Declan held up a finger. "The blob might be turkey."

"Now that that the ear showed up, that's looking a little less likely," said Charlotte.

Carolina slapped the counter. "What is *wrong* with you people? Why are you all so calm about this? There has to be a body in the house *somewhere*."

Mariska put a hand on her sister's shoulder. "Charlotte said the cats are bringing things in from somewhere outside. Maybe a shark attack victim washed up on shore?"

Charlotte chuckled. "Sure. And he threw his own finger in the trash before the cats carted him away, piece by piece."

"The trashcan discovery definitely implies some intent," said Seamus.

"And if it hadn't been for the freak freeze that kept the bag stuck to the bottom of that can, that finger would be at the dump by now. We lucked out there."

"Did we, though?" asked Declan.

"I'm going to go lie down for a bit," said Carolina.

Chuck stood from where he had been squatting, painting near the floor trim. "Me too."

"Finish painting," barked Carolina without looking at him.

Chuck sighed and resumed his work.

Mariska, Darla, and Bob wandered away to resume their own painting chores.

Charlotte looked at Seamus. "We need to search the grounds, but I can tell you, it's a mess out there right now."

"I know. I went out while you were gone."

"You did? Find anything?"

"I found contractor bags make pretty good slickers."

"I'm sorry I missed that. Did you find a *body*?"

"No. I searched the yard, the dunes, and what's left of the beach. Any cat prints leading from the house have been washed out. Tide might have taken everything else away."

"The neighbors have three cats, but there was no easy way to check their paws for paint. I only saw one of them, and he didn't seem particularly friendly."

"Sounds like a cat. Chances are pretty good that they're our guys. I'll roll over and check their yard."

Charlotte retrieved her phone and flipped through the apps. "Weather says there's a break in the rain coming later this afternoon. Maybe we could look again then."

Seamus started up the stairs. "Sounds like a plan. In the meantime, I'll knock out the plumbing."

"You're working on the upstairs sinks now?" asked Charlotte.

He turned and winked. "As far as you know."

Charlotte lingered in the kitchen, watching Declan and Chuck paint. She was trying to look *available* to help without actually inquiring if any was needed. She lifted the glass top to the butter dish and stared at the bits of *someone*.

Mariska was right. They were getting a little stinky.

She felt as if they were trapped in an Agatha Christie novel, only in *reverse*. Instead of *And Then There Were None*, they were in *And Then There Were SOME.* Maybe by the time they were done collecting parts, they'd have a whole other person they could cart back to Florida with them.

She was about to put the cover on the butter dish when the blob caught her eye, *AR*, stamped on its puckered flesh.

What if that isn't a turkey inspection stamp but a tattoo?

She'd seen a tattoo like that.

Mr. Marino on the beach.

His chest had an eagle with U.S. ARMY written on a banner held in its claws.

A-R-m-y.

Dinah didn't mention Mr. Marino while listing the occupants of each room.

Mr. Marino was gone.

Dead, gone...

She looked at the little pile of flesh.

Or maybe *found.*

CHAPTER FOURTEEN

Charlotte went upstairs and found Seamus parked in front of the television in the master bedroom, watching soccer.

"How's the plumbing going?" she asked.

"Better than Man City's going, I can tell you that. Man U is routing them."

"So you're a Man City fan?"

Seamus scoffed. "No. I'm disappointed they're not *both* losing. I'm Irish."

Charlotte watched the game for a moment. "I don't really know all the rules in soccer, so I won't pretend I know what's going on."

Seamus grimaced. "And *I* won't pretend I'm actually working on the plumbing."

Charlotte lingered, watching the screen until Seamus squinted at her.

"For someone who doesn't know anything about Premier League football, you seem awfully interested. That means one of two things."

She cocked an eyebrow. "Yes?"

"Either you're trying to get out of work, or you want to ask me something."

"You forgot option three."

"What's that?"

"Both."

"Ah. What's up?"

"I need your help. I need you to seduce a nurse."

"Done. Anything else?"

"Very funny. I was looking at that piece of flesh we found, and it has "A-R" tattooed on it. Next door, there was a photo of an old man with an Army tattoo on his chest."

"And you think he's the one leaving bits of himself all over the place?"

"Could be. I told you something seemed off with those people. Maybe they killed him. Maybe he wandered off, and they've been trying to hide the fact that they lost him."

"How do either of those scenarios end up with me sweet talking a nurse? You want me to find out what she knows?"

"Yes, but more than that, I want you to distract her. I'm thinking about inviting the neighbors over."

"For some meat, I assume."

"Naturally. And while Mariska and Darla are stuffing them with fifty-seven different versions of cow, I'll go next door and take a photo of that old soldier's picture so we can compare his tattoo to the stamp on the blob. Maybe I'll snoop around and see if I can find his death records."

"You think they'll leave the nurse behind to man the ship?"

She nodded. "The residents aren't spry enough to swing by for snacks. Someone has to stay there."

He nodded. "Think they'll bite?"

"Everybody loves meat snacks."

"True."

"Plus, the one woman I told you about, Dinah, all but invited herself over. I'm pretty sure Emmitt follows her lead."

Seamus shrugged. "I'm in. Clear it with the party

planning committee."

"That's my next stop."

Charlotte trotted downstairs and found Mariska and Darla on the sofa in the big room, watching the rest of the men paint. They'd covered the furniture and floor with plastic drop cloths, and every movement elicited a symphony of crackling noises.

Turbo sat on Darla's lap, oblivious to the racket. Abby and Izzy lay stretched on the floor, both dogs cracking open an eye as Charlotte entered before returning to their naps.

Carolina sat on an uncovered chair looking sleepy, her head tilted forward, her under-bite more pronounced than usual.

Charlotte flopped into a spare chair, plastic crinkling beneath her.

"Taking a break?" she asked.

Darla rolled her eyes. "Honey, I am *exhausted*. We're too old to be on the floor painting trim. I've pulled muscles where I didn't even know I had any."

Carolina was the only person not covered in paint splatter.

"You stayed impressively clean," said Charlotte.

Carolina opened her drooping lids to focus on her. "I'm chef and moral support."

"She doesn't deign to *paint*," said Darla, glancing at Carolina sidelong.

Carolina glowered back at her.

Still on the ladder, Declan strained to stroke the highest part of the wall. He peered down at Charlotte and mouthed the words *you so owe me.*

She chuckled and returned her attention to the ladies.

"It's a shame we're trapped here. We could have at *least* gone to dinner to break up the monotony."

"We could have walked on the beach with the dogs,"

agreed Darla.

"Exactly. You know who else is going stir-crazy? Our neighbors."

"You talked to them?" asked Mariska.

Charlotte nodded. "There's a woman named Dinah and the man who owns the place, Emmitt. There's a nurse, too, and the residents, of course, but they're mostly bed-bound."

"That's too bad," said Mariska.

Charlotte released an exaggerated sigh. "It's a shame. They're there, bored and stuck. We're here, bored and stuck with enough meat to feed an army..."

Mariska echoed her sigh. "Everybody's stuck—" Her eyes grew wide, and she gasped. "*We should invite them over.*"

Charlotte tried not to grin.

Fish on. She'd trolled and hooked Mariska.

"What's that?" she asked.

Mariska clapped her hands together. "The *neighbors.* We should have them over. Throw a little storm party."

"I don't want this place full of invalids," muttered Carolina.

"Oh, shush, Carolina. They won't bring over the patients. They have a nurse to watch over them."

Carolina pressed her lips tight. "I did buy cute little mini hamburger buns. I *could* make mini-burgers."

"Sliders," said Charlotte.

"Huh?"

"That's what they call little burgers. *Sliders.*"

Carolina scowled. "Why would they call them that?"

Charlotte shrugged, and Carolina rolled her eyes. "*Sliders.* That doesn't make any sense. I doubt they slide any easier than a normal-sized burger."

Charlotte turned her palms to the ceiling to indicate she was also unable to decipher the mysteries of burger nicknames.

Darla sighed. "It would be nice to get a break. And we do have to eat all this food."

"Agreed. A party is a great idea, Mariska," said Charlotte. *I'm so glad you thought of it.*

Charlotte leapt to her feet. "I'll go see if they'd be interested. What do you think? About four-thirty, five?"

Mariska's eyebrows shot skyward. "Oh, you're going to ask them *now*? Today?"

"Sure, why not?"

The ladies looked at one another, nodding. "Okay."

"I can have something ready by five," said Carolina.

"Great."

Charlotte donned her mix-and-match storm gear.

"Where you going?" asked Bob, carrying his paint roller to the sink to rinse it. Chuck puttered in from the living room to join him.

"We're going to have a storm party. I'm going over to invite the neighbors."

Chuck's eyes lit. "A party?"

Bob scowled. "You're going to invite the neighbors?"

She nodded.

He motioned to Chuck. "Hide the good stuff."

Chuck saluted and wandered off to squirrel away the best bourbon as Charlotte walked into the storm.

Wind battering her with rain, bits of plants, and sand, Charlotte picked her way through the mud to the front stairs of the nursing home.

She'd sold the ladies on the party. Now she had to ensure the party guests were willing.

Knocking, she turned her back toward the wind and waited for half a second. Dinah answered the door as if she'd been standing behind it for hours, hoping someone would knock.

"Hello, Charlotte. Good to see you again. Come in. Did you

lose power?"

Charlotte stepped out of the weather. "No. Better news than that. I was wondering if you would be interested in swinging by our house for a little storm party?"

Dinah's eyes opened wide. "A party? Oh, that would be wonderful. We're so terribly bored."

"Us too. Does five o'clock work?"

"That would be perfect."

"Everyone's invited, of course. You, Emmitt, Mr. Marino—"

Dinah tucked back her chin. "Mr. Marino? He's...he can't come."

Charlotte noted Dinah's stutter. The woman hadn't *said* Mr. Marino was dead, so perhaps he still had a room in the house? Her reaction to his name had been strange as if she'd been shocked to hear it, but Charlotte couldn't think of a polite way to probe for more information on Mr. Marino's status.

"I just meant everyone is invited."

Dinah nodded. "It will be Emmitt and me. The others don't do parties anymore, and Julia will stay to watch them."

Charlotte nodded and stepped back onto the porch. "Okay, we'll see you at five. Be careful coming over, though. It is a real mess out here."

"Should we bring anything?" asked Dinah.

Charlotte smiled and pulled her hood tight around her head.

"Anything but meat."

CHAPTER FIFTEEN

At five-thirty, Seamus knocked on the Elder Care-o-lina's door and waited as the wind whipped sand into his ears. He hunched over the cling-wrap-covered plate of food he held against his chest, attempting to protect it from the elements. Dinah and Emmitt had been back at their party for twenty minutes, and it was his turn to trigger the next phase of Charlotte's plan.

Distract the nurse with his irresistible charm and sex appeal.

A middle-aged woman with auburn hair answered the door and then ducked behind it as the wind and rain hit her face.

"Yes?" she asked, her eyes and forehead the only visible parts of her body, poking from behind the door.

"I thought you'd like a snack," said Seamus, raising his voice above the howling wind.

"*What?*"

"I said I thought you'd like a *snack*."

A roof shingle flew into the side of the house with a *bang!* and they both jumped.

The woman scowled. "Look, I don't—"

"Could I come in a second before I'm beheaded?" Seamus

asked, offering his most knee-weakening smile. Next to the *devilish wink*, the *knee-weakening smile* was his most effective maneuver.

The nurse sighed and took a step back. "Sure. Come on in."

Seamus stepped inside and, balancing the party plate in one hand, held out the other. "I'm Seamus, your neighbor this week."

"I'm Julia. You're the ones having the party? The ones with the crazy bus?"

He nodded. "Exactly. They let me know you were stuck here caring for the residents, and I thought, *That's not right.* So I braved the storm and brought you party food."

He thrust the plate at Julia, who took a moment to consider his offer and then accepted. She set the plate on a small table against the wall before her attention shifted to the floor at Seamus' feet. A steady pitter-patter of water dripped from his borrowed jacket, covering the entryway with a shallow puddle. The corners of Julia's mouth drooped a little farther with each drop.

Seamus glanced at his self-made lake. "Tell you what, let me clean that up."

He ripped off his jacket, hung it on a wooden peg embedded in the wall, stepped out of his shoes as if they were glued to the floor, and scooted for the kitchen at the back of the house.

"Hey, *wait*," called Julia.

He answered over his shoulder without pausing forward momentum. "Not a problem, just a sec...try one of those sliders."

Seamus flew into the kitchen, gliding on the tiles in his socks, and flipped the lock on the sliding glass door that mimicked the one they had back at their house. Charlotte stood tucked into the corner of the porch, wearing a trash bag secured with a belt around her middle. She looked like a wet cat.

Seamus paused long enough to wink.

Devilish or not, winks always made the ladies feel better.

Charlotte's dour demeanor remained unchanged.

Seamus heard Julia's footsteps headed his way and held up a finger, silently asking Charlotte to stay outside a little longer. He grabbed a roll of paper towels from a dispenser and bolted back toward the front door, nearly knocking over Julia as he re-entered the front hall.

"What are you doing?" she asked, looking past him into the kitchen.

He put an arm on her shoulder and led her back toward the front door. "Getting paper towels. I wanted to clean up that mess, and I hate to be a bother, but would you give me a hand with the puddle? My back is a mess."

Julia's scowled. "You went to get paper towels so that *I* can clean your puddle?"

"Yes, but with the backing of my full emotional support." He stopped beside the water and positioned her facing *away* from the kitchen.

With a huff, Julia pulled a wad of paper towels from the roll and lowered herself to her hands and knees. Seamus waited until she was engaged in the cleanup and then stepped back to find an angle that offered him a view of the back door. Finding it, he motioned to Charlotte that it was safe to enter.

From the corner of his eye, he saw Julia's head swivel toward him.

"What are you doing?" she asked.

He morphed his frantic motioning to Charlotte into an exaggerated stretch.

"Sometimes it helps if I do a little stretching before I do anything too strenuous," he said, adopting what he remembered as "warrior" pose. Back during his time in Miami, he'd attended a handful of yoga classes while tailing a woman cheating on her wealthy husband. In the end, he'd discovered that her yoga instructor was a downward *dog* indeed.

He caught a glimpse of Charlotte slipping into the house and dropped to his hands and knees beside Julia.

"Let me help you with that. I think my back can handle it now," he said loudly, hoping to cover any noise Charlotte's entry might make. He chattered about the amazing ability of water to warp wood and yet keep it afloat.

"How is it that a window leak can ruin a hardwood floor in minutes, but wooden boats last for years?"

"I'm sure I don't know," said Julia, attempting to rise to her feet.

He pulled her back down under the guise of toppling.

"Sorry, lost my balance," he said, retracting his hand.

Her lips pressed into a white, humorless line, Julia stood. Seamus did the same and cocked his head to listen. He heard nothing. He guessed Charlotte had made it safely into the house.

"I should probably get back to work," said Julia.

He nodded toward the plate of food sitting on the foyer table.

"Did you try the sliders? They're great."

"No. I just had lunch. In fact, I was about to watch a movie."

Seamus thrust his hands in his pockets and rocked back on his heels. "Oh yeah? What movie?"

Julia took a deep breath. She seemed very aware—and very annoyed—that he wasn't eager to leave.

"*The Notebook*," she answered as if someone was pulling the words from her mouth.

Seamus gasped and slapped his hand over his heart. "Oh, isn't that just the most *amazing* movie?" He softened his expression to show he'd been nearly moved to tears by the mere mention of the film.

Julia's expression twisted into a knot of confusion.

"It's my favorite," she said, looking at him as if she'd just noticed him standing there. "You're telling me *you* like it?"

He rolled his eyes. "*Like* it? Are you kidding? I *love* it."

The corner of Julia's mouth curled into a smile.

Seamus grinned.

Gotcha.

"I didn't think *men* liked that movie," she added.

He straightened and pounded his breast with one fist like an agitated silverback gorilla. "I'm *all* man, and I can tell you, I *love* that movie. But how can you stand it?"

"What? The movie?"

"The *crying*. I just cry for hours every time I see it."

She raised her open hand to her own chest. "I *know*. It's the most heartbreaking thing. But Ryan Gosling is so...so—"

"*Dreamy*," suggested Seamus.

"*Yes*." She giggled. "A little young for me, though."

"Nonsense. Now let me ask you. Did you see Nicholas Sparks' *The Longest Ride*?"

Julie's eyes lit. "I did."

"Well, you know, I haven't. Would you mind giving me a quick rundown?"

"Won't I ruin it for you?"

"No, no, not at all. I like knowing—"

Julia opened her mouth to launch into the retelling of the cowboy romance when a rustling sound at the top of the stairs caused her to freeze and cock her head.

Seamus pegged the noise as the rustling of a trash bag worn as a rain jacket by a person *trying* to be quiet. He coughed loudly and knocked his jacket off the peg of the coat rack.

"Did you hear something upstairs?" asked Julia, her face turning toward the second floor like a sunflower seeking out the morning sun.

"Hear something? No. Was it me? I coughed and, oh, I dropped my jacket..."

Julia shook her head. "No. What I heard came from *upstairs*. Give me a second. I need to check on the residents."

"No." Seamus touched her upper arm, and she shot him a look. He retracted his hand as if she were a hungry alligator. "I mean, if you *have* to. Of course. You have to make sure everyone is safe. It's just...I was getting over-excited about hearing your breakdown of *The Longest Ride*."

Julia stared at him a moment, a smile inching back to her lips.

"I have to go check. I'll be right back."

"Are you sure?" he asked.

"Yes. I'm sorry."

She started up the stairs.

"I'll wait here for you!" screamed Seamus at the top of his lungs. "I'll wait downstairs while you go upstairs and check on the residents because you thought you heard a noise!"

Julia paused and peered down at him from her spot at the banister railing.

"Why are you screaming?" she asked.

He scowled. "Was I loud?"

"Very."

"Sorry. I had the mumps as a kid. Affected my hearing. Sometimes I have a little trouble with volume control."

She nodded and continued up the stairs.

"Anyway, I'll be down here while you check up there!" he screamed one last time.

Seamus held his breath, waiting for a commotion to break out upstairs. After a few minutes, Julia appeared on the stairs once more.

"All well?" he asked.

She nodded. "I guess it *was* one of the residents."

Seamus glanced upstairs.

Crinkly Charlotte must be in a good hiding spot.

He looked at the door. Leaving Charlotte alone in the house with old bat-eared Julia didn't seem right. He needed to stay and run tackle for her.

He licked his lips and gave the nurse his most sincere stare. "Hey, I don't want to be too forward, but do you think I could catch a little of that movie with you?"

"You want to watch *The Notebook*?"

"Yes. I'm not a big party person. I'd much rather be here with you than making small talk next door."

Julia beamed, and she clasped her hands together beneath her chin like a schoolgirl. "Oh, I'd *love* the company. You wouldn't believe how they treat me here."

"Not good bosses?"

"They treat me like I'm *staff*."

Seamus paused, unsure how to respond. "But, you *are* staff, aren't you?"

Julia sighed. "Yes. But no one wants to be *treated* like staff."

"Right. Right. You're like one of the family, right?"

Julia's eyes widened, and she pointed at him. "*Yes*. You understand."

He patted her on the shoulder. "Of course, I do, dear."

Beaming, Julia headed for the television in the living room, and Seamus glanced upstairs. Charlotte peered down at him, half her face half visible at the corner of the hallway wall. Waving his hand, he confirmed she could see him and hooked his thumb toward the front door. She'd need to sneak out the front door. Once he and Julia stationed themselves in front of the television, they'd be too close to the back door for Charlotte to escape the way she'd entered.

Charlotte nodded and ducked out of sight.

Seamus clapped his hands together as the TV unpaused and *The Notebook* began to play.

"You can tell me about *The Longest Ride* during the slow parts."

Julia giggled and slapped a hand on his knee. "As if there *are* slow parts."

His eye dropped to her hand, which remained resting on his lower thigh.

Once again, he'd underestimated the power of his charm.

Easy, boyo. Dial it back. Don't break the lass' heart.

CHAPTER SIXTEEN

Half an Hour Earlier.

Munching on a mini-hamburger, Charlotte made eye contact with Seamus and gave him the signal to head to Elder Care-o-lina.

He nodded and strolled from the room.

Dinah and Emmitt had been at the beach house for their impromptu meat party for twenty minutes. They'd brought deviled eggs and cream cheese stuffed celery. Charlotte wasn't sure how they'd made the snacks on such short notice unless they possessed the same superpower she'd thought reserved for Pineapple Port residents. Back at home, she could invite *any* older person to a party, and five minutes later, they'd appear with deviled eggs and cream cheese celery. She'd thought it was Florida magic but now suspected it was old-people magic, regardless of state.

Not that she minded. She *loved* deviled eggs, and celery made a fine vehicle for a blob of cream cheese.

Emmitt had joined Bob, Seamus, Declan, and Chuck for a bourbon. She noted that the Florida group had enjoyed Emmitt's company enough to offer him the *good* stuff for his second splash. He had no idea just how honored he should feel.

Dinah was regaling Carolina, Mariska, and Darla with stories of her youth in Iowa. Apparently, she'd been Corn Queen of her town three years running, a record that still stood.

With everyone occupied, Charlotte put phase one of their plan into action by giving Seamus the signal. Once he left, she noticed the box of contractor bags Seamus had borrowed from earlier and grabbed one to serve as a slicker.

"What are you up to?" said a voice behind her.

She shook and whirled to find Declan behind her.

"Were you a ninja in another life? You almost gave me a heart attack."

"You've been slowly backing out of the room for the last ten minutes. We've been together long enough that I can tell when you're up to something."

"I'm that predictable?"

Declan stared at her, and Charlotte frowned.

"Shoot. I like to think I'm a little more mysterious than that."

"Let's say you're *predictably mysterious*."

Charlotte grinned. "I'll take it." She booped him on the tip of the nose with her fingertip because she knew he hated it, and she hadn't liked being called predictable.

Grr.

He wrinkled his nose. "Don't try to distract me with cutesy. What are you up to?"

"I *love* how you know me so well."

"Uh huh. I know Seamus, too, and he's AWOL, so I know you're both up to something. Probably the *same* thing."

She glanced back into the living room to be sure all parties were engaged before pulling Declan close. Open-concept houses were great for entertaining but terrible for clandestine meetings: historically, the second most important function of a kitchen after food preparation.

"You know the blob I found with the tattoo on it?" she whispered.

"The barfed turkey?"

"That's just it. I think it might be a *person's* tattoo, and I might have seen the person in a photo over at the nursing home. He had an *army* tattoo. *A-R*, like the blob."

"You think they killed one of their residents and buried the body out back?"

"I don't know. But I do think our neighbors are up to *something*. Seamus and I are going to take a little peek while they're *here*."

"Is that why we're having this party? To lure them out of the house?"

Charlotte squinted one eye. "Maybe."

"But wasn't the party Mariska's idea? Wait. *No.* I remember you talking to her while I was painting. You made her *think* it was her idea."

Charlotte shrugged a shoulder.

He took a deep breath. "Remind me not to mess with you. You might be a witch." Declan glanced in the direction of the Elder Care-o-lina. "Isn't there a nurse over there? And a bunch of residents?"

"That's where Seamus comes in. He's going to keep the nurse enthralled with his sparkling personality."

Declan nodded. "He *is* a charming bastard for the first hour or so."

"Exactly. I'm going to sneak in the back and take a photo of the picture I saw on the wall there. Maybe look around a bit."

"And you know this guy in the photo is a patient?"

"Yes. Or *ex*-patient. Dinah implied he was dead or gone, or at the very least, unable to come to the party. Who knows? I might open a door and find him sleeping soundly in a room.

That's what this mission is for—to find out."

Declan frowned. "I should never have introduced you to Seamus. You're as crazy as he is."

She glanced at the guests to be sure they were still locked in conversation. "I have to get going before we run out of sliders and bourbon."

Declan sighed. "Well, *jeeze*, I want to play, too. What can I do?"

"Keep an eye on these guys. If they move to leave and we're not back, do your best to keep them here or get a signal to us."

"Aye-aye," Declan saluted.

She rolled her eyes and grabbed a cap from the peg on the wall beside the backdoor. Opening the door to the back porch, she slipped outside as Declan did his best to block the view of her exit from the others.

Charlotte scurried down the stairs and, using the porch as an umbrella, took a moment to slip the contractor bag over her head and poke her skull through the bottom seam. Getting her head through was harder than she'd expected; she had to slice it with a fingernail to get the gap started.

It was almost as if trash bags weren't made to be worn.

The bag was wide and flappy in the wind. She removed the belt from her jeans and tied it around the outside of the bag to secure her makeshift poncho. She felt ridiculous, but both Chuck's and Carolina's jackets were much too large on her, and Seamus had taken the spare. No matter. Better to be unhampered. She wanted to move like the *wind*.

She made her way to the next yard, mud once again threatening to suck the boots from her feet. Climbing the back stairs of Elder Care-o-lina's porch, she tried the door, expecting Seamus to have unlocked it by then.

It was locked.

She positioned herself out of sight, occasionally peeking

for a sign of Seamus. After four peeps from her spot, she spotted Seamus sliding on his socks toward the back door. The latch clicked, and he winked at her.

Very funny.

He knew she looked like a wet cat.

She was about to enter when Seamus held up a finger, silently asking her to wait.

She ducked back into her hiding spot, rain streaming down her face.

A moment later, he disappeared toward the front of the house. She stared at the spot where he'd disappeared until he appeared once more, beckoning for her to enter.

She eased open the door, walked out of her muddy boots, and stepped inside. Out in the foyer, she heard Seamus and Julia talking.

She paused.

Did I just hear Seamus call Ryan Gosling 'dreamy?'

She cocked her head to listen as she moved toward the stairs.

Are they talking about The Notebook?

Baffled, she fought to ignore her curiosity and crept up the stairs to the second floor. She only moved when she heard voices, hoping the chatter would cover the sound of floorboards creaking.

Safe in the upstairs hallway, she hurried to the photo of Mr. Marino on the beach. The print of his tattoo did seem similar to the lettering on the flesh they'd found. Removing her phone from her pocket, she took a few pictures of the tattoo so she could compare them back home. Mr. Marino was face-forward in the photograph, so she couldn't see if his *ears* appeared familiar.

She glanced down the hall toward Emmitt's room. Dinah hadn't opened that door during the tour, and she couldn't help but wonder what might be hiding there. Maybe he kept the death records there. Certainly, Emmitt wouldn't have a document that said, *killed Mr. Marino today, buried his body in the backyard,* but if she could find some mention of what *officially* happened to him, it could be a starting point for a storyline that ended with Marino's ear in a sandwich baggie.

She took a step toward Emmitt's room and hit the squeakiest floorboard in the history of houses. The creak sprung like a trap, and she threw herself against the wall, her plastic bag coat rustling, making even more noise.

She hugged herself and froze.

A moment later, Seamus' voice rose from downstairs, much louder than the conversation she'd heard before.

"I'll wait here for you!"

Charlotte swallowed, frightened to move.

"I'll wait downstairs while you go upstairs and check on the residents because you thought you heard that noise!" screamed Seamus.

Not subtle, but effective. There was no doubt that Julia was on her way to investigate.

She had to move.

A door in the hallway opened, and a woman with a halo of white curls peered out.

"Who are you?" she asked upon spotting Charlotte.

Charlotte heard Julia hit the stairs and panicked, looking from the old woman to the stairs and back.

She had to do *something.*

She locked eyes with the woman.

What was her name? She loves Murder She Wrote. I remember that bit. What is it...what is it...

"Grace!"

The woman smiled. "Yes?"

Charlotte shot into Grace's room, pulling the elderly woman in with her and shutting the door behind them. "Hi, Grace. I'm glad I found you. Quick, follow me."

"Why are you whispering?" asked Grace.

Charlotte could hear Julia's footsteps on the stairs.

She took Grace's hand and tried to look as serious as possible. "Jessica Fletcher sent me."

Another little-known advantage of growing up in a retirement community: knowledge of *Murder She Wrote.*

Grace gasped. "Jessica sent you?"

Charlotte nodded, aware that at any moment, Julia would open the door. She dropped to her knees on the opposite side of Grace's bed, laid on her back, and began shimmying beneath it.

She left her face sticking out, and Grace stared down at her, seemingly baffled but unalarmed.

Charlotte felt terrible lying to the woman, but she was out of ideas. "Grace, I'm on a case, and I need your help. I need to hide for a little bit. Don't tell anyone I'm here. Can you do that for me?"

Grace nodded. "Oh I can. *I can.*"

Charlotte withdrew her head like a turtle into its shell, her nose grazing Grace's mattress support slats.

"What's the case?" asked Grace.

Charlotte poked out her head again. "Um, *Russians.* There's a Russian spy on the loose." She grimaced, suspecting that Jessica Fletcher didn't deal in international politics. She made a mental note to watch some refresher episodes of *Murder She Wrote* in case she ever found herself in a similar situation. There were probably fifty people back in Pineapple Port who'd been given the complete DVD boxed set at one time or another.

At the mention of Russians, Grace's lips formed an *O,* and her eyes grew wide.

Ah, Grace seems impressed by the Russian story. That's all that matters.

There was a knock on the door. Charlotte thrust out her arm and put her index finger over her lips, asking Grace to be quiet. Grace nodded.

Charlotte pulled her head back under the bed and held her breath. Partially to be quiet. Partially because she could barely breathe, squeezed beneath the bed.

Grace climbed onto her mattress, and Charlotte turned her head as dust rained on her face.

Don't think about sneezing. Don't think about sneezing—

"Grace?" called a voice from the hall.

"Yes?"

"It's Julia. Can I come in?"

Charlotte heard the door open and saw Julia's foot enter the room.

"Were you just in the hallway?" asked Julia.

There was a long pause.

From her hiding place, Charlotte grimaced, trying her best to telepathically send a request to Grace.

Please say yes, Grace.

"Yes," said Grace.

Charlotte blinked. *It worked. Am I telepathic?*

"Did you need something?" continued Julia.

"No."

"Everything's okay?"

"Yes. There aren't any Russians."

There was a pause, and Charlotte winced again, hoping that Julia wouldn't feel the need to delve into the Russian situation.

Julia cleared her throat. "Okay, well, don't wander around. If you need anything, hit the buzzer, okay?"

"I will."

Julia closed the door, and Charlotte breathed again. She squirmed out from under the bed. The fit had been tight.

It might be a good idea to stay away from the cream cheese celery for a bit.

She couldn't be responsible for her behavior around

deviled eggs.

Grace hung over the side of the bed, staring at Charlotte as she shimmied free.

"How was that?" she asked.

Charlotte stood and brushed her face clean. "Fantastic. Perfect. Thank you *so* much. You've saved the free world."

Grace sat up and grabbed Charlotte's upper arm, her eyes darting to her door. "Is she one of them?" she whispered.

Charlotte followed her gaze. "Who? Julia?"

Grace nodded.

"Oh, no. She's not Russian. She's on our side."

Grace sighed. "Good. I like her."

The old woman leaned back. She closed her eyes the moment her head hit the pillow.

"Tell Jessica I said *hi*," she mumbled.

"I will."

"I'm going to take a nap now."

"Okay."

Charlotte patted Grace's hand and tiptoed to the door. Cracking it open, she glanced down the hallway.

Julia was gone.

Downstairs, she heard Julia and Seamus resuming their conversation.

Charlotte chewed her lip for a moment. She still wanted to check Emmitt's room, but Julia had shaken her nerves.

Be brave. This is your one chance.

She took a deep breath and slipped into the hall, quietly closing Grace's door behind her.

Laying her fingers on Emmitt's doorknob, she gave it a gentle twist.

Unlocked.

She let herself inside.

Emmitt's room was unremarkable, featuring a bed, a chest of drawers, and a large, roll-top desk. She opened the desk drawers, finding them largely empty but for one clearly designated for snacks. It spilled over with half-eaten bags of chips and other salty treats.

She rolled open the top of the desk. Piles of canceled checks and invoices covered the workspace. Most of the checks appeared to be from D.F.A.S., *Defense Finance and Accounting Service*. Dinah had mentioned that the Elder Care-o-lina housed many veterans, and Charlotte guessed the residents' pensions were sent directly to the house. She flipped through them until the name *Anthony Marino* caught her eye.

The check was dated for the previous week.

Mr. Marino is alive?

She spotted what looked like patient files with names on the tabs and shuffled through them until she found Anthony Marino. The file contained a medical history, his original application to the home, and weekly records of his condition. She glanced over the last few months of entries. The notations were fairly detailed for his first years. It appeared a few months prior he'd started refusing to eat. Soon after, the notes became more and more vague. The last six months said nothing but *no change*.

Charlotte glanced at the date of the last log.

It was dated three months *in the future.*

Her brow furrowed.

Something didn't add up. The check said Mr. Marino was still alive, but the file implied they'd stopped thinking about him. They were going through the motions of reporting his status—so much so they'd recorded the equivalent of *ditto* three months into the future.

She felt certain Mr. Marino was dead.

But Emmitt had never reported him dead.

He was pretending to care for Marino while collecting his government checks. Meanwhile, another veteran occupied the room Marino left behind and even more occupied the rooms nearby.

All of whom might one day have unreported deaths…

Charlotte retrieved her phone and took a picture of the check and the medical reports. She was about to close the desk when she paused to consider the piece of furniture itself.

Something is very familiar about this desk.

Mariska had a friend with a similar piece of furniture. Charlotte remembered the woman showing her the secret drawer it possessed. As a girl of ten, she'd been fascinated by secret hiding places and had *begged* Mariska to buy her a desk like it for Christmas.

She never did get the desk. By the time Christmas rolled around, she'd been obsessed with something new. But she still remembered that secret drawer.

In rapid succession, Charlotte opened all the small drawers lining the back of the desk to check their depth. If one was short, it implied something was behind it.

They all appeared uniform.

Hm. Ah well.

She put her hand on the handle to pull down the roll-top and paused once more.

Columns. A small, closet-like compartment sat in the back center of the desktop. On either side of it, decorative columns protruded from the wood. She pinched one and pulled.

It slid.

The column was attached to a hollow box. She pulled it out like sliding a novel from a bookshelf and peered inside.

Empty.

Shoot.

She replaced it and tugged the other column. Inside this hollow box was something small and shiny. She turned it upside-down, and the object dropped into her palm.

A key.

It looked like a house key.

Downstairs she heard the television spring to life. On a whim, she dropped the key into her jeans pocket and slid the column box back into place.

She needed to go. She was pushing her luck lingering so long. Seamus would lose his mind wondering if she'd made it to safety. Who knew how long he could continue his charade? She knew his Irish charm had limits. Even a Leprechaun could only distract someone for so long.

She crept to the door and peeked outside. No one was in the hall.

Scurrying to the steps, she did her best to avoid the creaky spots and peered downstairs.

Seamus stood in the foyer below. He spotted her and motioned to the front door.

She nodded and ducked back out of sight.

Seamus' voice soon reached her ears, sounding farther away than where she'd seen him standing. Charlotte reasoned he'd sneaked to the foyer to look for her and then returned to his place in the living room. It sounded as if he and Julia were watching television.

Seeing her chance, she bolted down the stairs as fast as she could without sounding like a herd of cattle and slipped out the front door.

On the porch, she ran halfway down the stairs and then jogged back up again. She pulled the key from her pocket and slipped it into the door lock.

It fit.

She tried to turn it.

Nothing.

It wasn't the key to their front door.

That narrowed it down to a million possibilities.

CHAPTER SEVENTEEN

Gritting her teeth against the cold, Charlotte pulled off her socks and circled to the back of the Elder Care-o-lina, freezing mud squishing between her toes.

She found her shoes still stuffed in the corner of the porch where she'd left them. She slipped into them and glanced through the glass into the house. Seamus and Julia were on the sofa, watching a movie she recognized.

The Notebook.

That explained a little.

Something about Julia's sitting position caught her attention, and she stood on her toes to get a better view.

Julia's hand was resting on Seamus' knee.

Okaaay.

It was definitely time to go. She wasn't sure how committed Seamus was to their plan, and she didn't want to know.

She ran back to the vacation house and, after throwing out her makeshift jacket and rinsing her feet in the bathroom sink, rejoined the party.

Declan seemed relieved to see her.

"You're back," he said as she grabbed a deviled egg.

"I am."

"I think they're getting ready to leave. I was starting to panic." He eyed her from head to toe. "You're wet."

"It's raining."

"True. That'll do it. Did you find anything?"

"Maybe. I'll tell you in a bit."

"Where's Seamus?"

"If I had to guess, I'd say *taking one for the team.*"

Charlotte reached for a cream cheese celery. She stared at the treat in her hand, recalling her time beneath Grace's bed. Glancing to see if anyone was watching, she put the celery back on the plate.

Her plan had been to stuff her face and then probe Emmitt and Dinah for more information on Mr. Marino. As she set down the celery, Dinah stood and began her goodbyes.

Darn. Her lust for cream cheese had lost her the chance to interrogate the guests.

But more importantly, were they going to take back the uneaten deviled eggs?

"I'll clean your dishes and bring them back to you," said Mariska to Dinah.

Charlotte smiled. Mariska always had a ready excuse for keeping food. Offering to clean the guests' dishes ensured that the eggs would stay with them.

Dinah and Emmitt left amid a flurry of goodbyes and hugs. Most of the hugs came from Emmitt, who seemed extremely friendly and a little unsteady on his feet after his time visiting with the Bourbon Club.

"Where did you go?" asked Darla, poking Charlotte on the shoulder after the guests had left. With her other hand, she snatched a deviled egg from Mariska as she walked by with the platter.

Charlotte put her own hand on her midsection. "Had a little stomach issue."

Darla arched an eyebrow as she bit into the egg. "I wonder why? I can't believe there are any of these left."

"I didn't have *that* many deviled eggs. And please, my body is just dying for something *not* in the meat group at this point."

"I think eggs *are* in the meat group," said Declan.

Charlotte scowled. "I had celery, too."

A wind whipped through the house, and all heads turned as Seamus entered through the backdoor. He shook out his jacket, hung it on a peg, and slipped out of his boots.

"Where were you?" asked Darla, carrying used cups into the kitchen.

"Went for a walk," he said without a moment's hesitation.

"In this weather?"

He nodded and thumped himself on the chest with his fist. "Brisk. Reminds me of Ireland."

He moved to Charlotte and Declan. "Hey. How'd it go?"

"Why do you look like you've been crying?" asked Declan.

Seamus sniffed. "Damn *Notebook*. Ending gets me every time."

"You really have to find yourself some male friends," said Charlotte.

Declan frowned. "What am *I*?"

"I mean, *besides* his nephew."

Seamus shrugged. "I can't help it. I love the ladies."

Charlotte smirked. "Looked like she loved you, too."

"It was totally innocent. Sweet Julia just needed a little attention. A little human touch."

Declan's lip curled. "Ew." He turned to Charlotte. "Can you say what you found now?"

"And change the subject?"

"*Exactly.*"

Charlotte fished for her phone as she told them how

Emmitt was receiving checks for Mr. Marino and that she felt sure he'd been dead for some time.

"So those body parts *are* his," said Declan.

"Likely." Charlotte manifested the photo of Mr. Marino on the beach and zoomed in on his tattoo. She moved to the butter-dish coffin, which had been artfully hidden from the guests behind a loaf of bread and a dishtowel. She compared the letters in the photo to those on the blob.

"It's hard to tell. They're so wrinkly. They seem pretty close..."

"Which are wrinkly? The letters on the blob or the ones on the old man's chest?" asked Seamus, elbowing Declan in the ribs.

"Ow. Cut it out."

"What are you three up to?" asked Carolina as she passed, carrying an empty plate to the sink. "Besides not helping to clean up."

Charlotte closed the butter dish. "Nothing."

Carolina glowered at them. "You're up to something. You and your *detecting*."

"What could they be detecting here?" asked Mariska, following close behind her sister with the remainder of the celery.

Carolina pointed. "There's a dang finger in the butter dish, Mariska. *That* would be a good place to start detecting."

"Did you happen to show our guests the butter coffin?" asked Charlotte.

"Oh lordy, no," said Darla, chuckling. "I'm pretty sure Martha Stewart's handbook has a whole chapter on never showing body parts to your guests."

"Dead or alive," mumbled Declan.

Charlotte covered the dish. "I'm sorry. Do you need help cleaning up?"

Carolina huffed a laugh. "The last time I pulled a fork

from your kitchen drawer, there was a piece of dried lettuce stuck to one of the prongs. I think we can handle this."

Charlotte's nose wrinkled. "Well, that's embarrassing."

Carolina winked at her, and Charlotte left the kitchen on the off-chance they reconsidered her offer to help.

Declan and Seamus were sitting in the living room, and she joined them.

"So what do we do now?" asked Declan.

"We don't have proof that Marino is actually dead," said Seamus.

"Unless you count a finger, an ear, and a chunk of chest," said Charlotte.

Seamus shook his head. "We don't *know* that's him, and wouldn't you know, I forgot to bring my DNA test kit."

"I think when people go missing, and people *parts* start appearing, there's a pretty good chance those things are related," said Declan.

Seamus shrugged. "Maybe. From what you said, Marino might not be the only one, either. Or it could be the partner, James. They say he's *gone* but maybe *missing* is more like it.

Charlotte nodded. Something about the resident's rooms had struck her as odd. She hadn't seen any personal items on the residents' doors or on their nightstands—no drawings from grandkids or other things that implied someone might miss that person after they died.

"They might specialize in veterans who don't have families in order to more easily claim their benefits," she suggested.

"That would be the way to do it," agreed Seamus.

"Once the storm ends, the cops can DNA test the ear. Then we'll know," said Declan.

Seamus nodded. "In theory. But if Marino doesn't have anyone missing him, they'd have nothing to compare the test to. No kids, no grandkids—"

"No hairs from his hairbrush. I'm sure all his stuff is long gone," added Charlotte.

"Probably. Which means unless he was a criminal in his twilight years and already in the database, they'll be out of luck."

Declan frowned. "How can people be forgotten like this? Doesn't the government check on people?"

Seamus shook his head. "Only family cares where you are when you're old."

"Sad."

"Depressing," agreed Charlotte. She slapped her hand to her pocket. "I almost forgot. I found this in Emmitt's desk, tucked in a hidden compartment."

She pulled out the key and held it out for the others to see.

"What do you think that's for?" asked Declan.

"I don't know. Not their front or back door. I tried."

Seamus sat back in his seat, interlacing his fingers and resting his hands on his chest. "There's another thing that's eatin' at me."

"What's that?" asked Charlotte.

"You found the finger in *our* trash. I found that tooth in *our* drain."

"Cats didn't do *that*," said Declan.

"No. Which means—"

Charlotte finished his thought. "They're using this house to cut up the bodies before ditching them somewhere?"

"Sweet dreams," mumbled Declan.

Seamus sat forward again and plucked the key from her fingers. He stood and walked toward the front door.

"Come with me."

Declan and Charlotte followed him into the foyer. Seamus went outside and shut the door behind him.

"Lock it," he called back to them.

Declan locked the door. They heard the doorknob rattle, and then the door swung open as Seamus reentered.

"It's the key to *this* house," said Charlotte.

"When no one was renting, this was the perfect place to cut up the body," said Declan.

Seamus handed her the key. "This means they could have come here and chopped us up in our sleep at any time."

Charlotte bit her lip. "Whatever you do, don't tell the others; we'll have a mutiny on our hands. They'll be building escape boats out of the walls."

"Is Emmitt going to miss that key?" asked Declan.

"I don't know, but they're not getting it back," said Charlotte.

Seamus closed and locked the door as Charlotte's gaze settled on the stairs. "I need to get that ear out of my bedroom and move it down here with the rest of the bits. Darla will kill me if she finds it up there."

Seamus nodded and pulled the tooth he'd found from his pocket, still wrapped in its baggie.

"We're going to need a bigger butter dish."

CHAPTER EIGHTEEN

Seamus lay in his little boy bed, staring at the ceiling. He couldn't stop thinking about the tooth he'd found in the sink. No one simply *lost* a tooth with that much gum tissue on it. Now that Charlotte showed him the key, he felt more certain than ever that their house had been used to dismember a body or two.

How hard could it be to prove it?

The neatest person in the world would have a hard time chopping up a corpse without leaving evidence behind.

Swinging his legs over the side of the bunk bed, Seamus dropped to the ground. He started out of the room and then stopped.

Should probably put on some pants.

Back at Declan's house, he had a tendency to walk around in his boxers, but there were ladies present here. He didn't want to drive them all mad with desire.

Seamus donned a pair of sweatpants and trotted down two flights of stairs to the utility room. Upon reaching the bottom stair of the lower level, he flipped on the light.

A squirrel sat on its haunches in the middle of the room, staring at him. He held something small and fleshy in his little paws.

Seamus put his hands on his hips, happy he'd pushed off blocking the hole to the outside. He'd hoped something might sneak in again and give them a chance to follow it back to the body.

"So it's *you*. You've been giving the cats a bad rap."

The squirrel blinked.

Seamus bent forward. "What are you trying to hide in here today?"

The squirrel turned and bolted behind the water heater. Seamus ran after it, unsure what he would do if he caught it. He imagined catching a squirrel was like tackling a living food processor, buck teeth tearing at everything within reach.

By the time he reached the hole in the wall, the furry rodent was gone.

Thank goodness.

He didn't really need to catch it. He needed to *follow* it.

Spinning a hundred and eighty degrees, Seamus snatched a flashlight from the workbench and bolted outside into the rain. The home's outdoor lighting illuminated the back yard, most of which lay beneath several inches of standing water. The only dry area was near the house, so he scanned that area, suspecting the squirrel would avoid the water if it could.

He caught a flash of movement at the far side of the patio area beneath the second-story porch and bolted in that direction.

Reaching the edge of the house, he found the area between their house and the Elder Care-o-lina spotted with sizeable puddles. In the ambient light cast by the security lamps, he watched the squirrel leap from island to island.

Seamus braced himself and jumped onto the nearest dry island, hoping the squirrel would lead him to its dead body buffet.

The rodent shot beneath an outdoor shower and

disappeared. Seamus leapt forward, mud squishing between his toes. His right foot landed, but as he dragged his left beside it, he realized the first had continued to slide without his permission.

He felt his center of balance tilting backward, past the point of no return.

Shite.

He hit the ground hard on his back, muddy water splashing around and over him like a damp fireworks display. Panting in shallow breaths, he lay there as the rain pelted his face.

His first attempt to rise elicited a painful twinge in his back. He yipped and settled back to the ground.

A strange calm washed over him. Lying flat and still in a mud puddle in the rain was much like meditating, but for the throbbing pain in his back.

Tilting his head to the side, he raised his flashlight and shone it under the outdoor shower. He could see where the wood had been chewed away on the opposite side, creating a makeshift door that led directly into the Elder Care-o-lina.

The squirrel hadn't led him to the body. He'd led him to his other hiding spot.

He switched off the flashlight and lay in the dark, thinking.

Unless...

Unless the body was *in the Elder Care-o-lina.*

With a cacophony of grunting and groaning, he struggled to his feet and hobbled back to the house. In their own outdoor shower, he rinsed off, gritting his teeth to keep from screaming at the cold. The water felt like ice pellets striking his naked torso, and he released a string of profanities beneath his breath—some familiar, some invented—all carrying the proper import.

With stiff, freezing fingers, he wrung out his shirt and retied his wet sweats as they fought to drop to his ankles. Having hips or a butt would've come in handy for keeping his soggy drawers around his waist, but he hadn't had either of those things in a long time.

Wiping his eyes and face, he went inside. The wet sweats clung to his legs, their clammy death grip making it difficult to move. Unable to bear the feel of them a moment longer, he untied them and let them drop to the ground with a wet slap. His boxer shorts traveled along with the sweats.

He noticed someone had brought the box of contractor bags downstairs. Grabbing one, he ripped a hole into the sealed bottom and poked his head through it.

The "hem" of his makeshift dress came to the middle of his thigh.

He shrugged.

Short hemlines are in this season.

He found an old hand cloth and dried the flashlight as he clomped to the main level. The flashlight had been the object of his desire all along before he'd been distracted by fuzzy rats.

Flipping on the light in the kitchen, he moved to the computer hutch and opened a drawer to retrieve a roll of clear packaging tape he'd noticed there earlier. He tore away a piece with his teeth and pasted it over the head of the flashlight. Taking a blue Sharpie pen from the desk drawer, he colored the tape. He repeated the process with another piece and another after that.

He switched on the flashlight to be sure he hadn't missed any spots and then turned off the lights.

Walking to the sink, he shone the blue light on the floor and counters. The white of the cabinets glowed beneath the beam.

Uh oh.

"What are you doing?" said someone.

Seamus turned the flashlight in the direction of the voice.

Declan stood at the edge of the kitchen, eyeing his uncle's trash bag dress.

"What the heck are you *wearing*?"

Seamus lifted the flashlight to his face, knowing his makeshift UV light would make his teeth and eyes glow.

"You've officially lost your mind," said Declan, flipping on the lights.

"I can imagine it looks that way."

"Where did you find a black light?"

"*UV* light. I made it."

"How is that possible?"

"With tape and a blue permanent marker."

"No kidding?" Declan turned the lights off again and took the flashlight from Seamus. He shone it on the cabinets, and their surface glowed.

Most of it.

"What's all this dark stuff?" he said, sweeping the flashlight back and forth. The white cabinets were splattered with dark spots that continued to the ground. It was harder to see them on the darker floor tiles, but it was clear that some of whatever had hit the cabinets had settled to the floor.

"I'm guessing blood," said Seamus.

Declan's head snapped up. "Seriously? I thought blood *glowed* beneath UV light. This is darker."

"That's TV stuff. You need luminol to make it glow."

Declan continued to sweep the light across the kitchen floor, discovering more smears and splatter. "This is *all* blood?"

"Maybe. Might be grease and spaghetti sauce, and who knows what, but I'm guessing blood. The patterns look very *killy*."

"Killy?"

"Like the patterns that happen when people are *killed*."

"Ah. *Killy* is an official detective term."

"Exactly."

Declan squatted and took a closer look at the floor. "It's smeared here."

"Where someone tried to clean it up."

Declan moved to the light switch and turned it on. The blood spots disappeared, the drops on the lower cabinets too fine to see in the light.

Seamus stood thinking while Declan stared at him.

"Should I ask about the trash bag dress you're wearing?" Declan asked as Seamus met his gaze.

"It's all the rage in Paris."

"Uh huh. What's wrong? You look stiff, too. You're kind of waddling."

Seamus rubbed the back of his neck and tried to stretch his back. "I ran after a squirrel I found downstairs and slipped and fell in the mud outside. The wet sweatpants were awful."

"You found a squirrel downstairs? You mean in the house?"

Seamus nodded. "We've been blaming the cats. Looks like it's the squirrels. Little bastard had a chunk of something too, but he took it with him."

"Maybe the cat was in the house trying to catch the squirrel."

"Maybe."

"Okay. I guess that explains your trash bag dress—though wouldn't it have been easier to go upstairs and change?"

"Too lazy to go upstairs and didn't want to do it naked anyway."

"Since when?" muttered Declan.

They stood in silence, staring at the floor.

"So chances are good that whoever owned that tooth you found was killed right here," said Declan.

"Probably."

"I take it we're going to keep this little nugget to ourselves for now. Other than Charlotte, of course?"

Seamus nodded. "This drastically changes the *five-second rule* around here."

"You mean the five seconds a piece of food is still edible once you've dropped it on the floor?"

"Yep."

Declan agreed. "I think this has changed that rule for me *permanently.*"

CHAPTER NINETEEN

Morning arrived, shedding light on yet another miserable day. Charlotte cupped her hands around her hot mug of coffee. She was starting to understand why so many northerners traveled to Florida in the winter.

She still didn't forgive them.

"What do we have on the docket today?" she asked from her seat at the kitchen table. She'd been toying with the idea of sleeping in, but Carolina had awoken early, and the whole house smelled like bacon. Fear of missing bacon had shot her out of bed like a cannon.

"Probably a nose. We find a darn body part every day," said Carolina, cracking an egg with gusto.

Charlotte shook her head. "I mean, *what's on the fix-it-up list*?"

Chuck sat across from her, reading a crime thriller that one of the previous renters had left behind. He glanced up and peered over his reading glasses at her. "Changing out hardware today. Kitchen cabinets, couple doorknobs, fix a stripped door hinge, painting more trim." He stretched his neck for a view of Darla, who sat at the computer desk, rolling through her Facebook timeline. "How much are we getting paid for this again?"

"For the umpteenth time, it's a *free vacation*," said Darla, staring through the sliding glass porch doors at the steady downpour. "Though I know it doesn't feel like it."

She returned her attention to the monitor where Brenda smiled, her ghost-white skin tone growing slightly darker in each photo as her tropical vacation progressed.

Chuck grimaced. "Look at that woman. We might have gotten the raw end of this deal."

"Ya think?" said Bob. Mariska had him cutting the tomatoes she'd brought from Florida for BLT sandwiches, sans L, thanks to Carolina's aversion to green foods.

Darla scrolled away from Brenda's photos. "The worst part is Brenda *tried* to cancel on me at the last second, and I wouldn't let her. After months of *begging* me for help, she said she'd decided to sell this place as-is. I told her plans were already made—too late to cancel, that I'd let you all down— blah, blah blah. What an idiot I was."

"Yep. Next time, *please*, let us all down," said Chuck, returning to his book.

Mariska placed a bacon and tomato sandwich on the desk beside Darla and patted her on the shoulder. "It's not your fault. You can't control the weather."

Darla nodded glumly and bit into her sandwich.

Mariska delivered Charlotte's meal next.

"Where's the salt?" asked Charlotte. On the table sat a lone pewter pepper grinder.

Mariska brought her a small, white plastic salt shaker. "The mate to that pepper is missing."

Charlotte used the salt and then grabbed the pepper. "That's too bad. This is a nice pepper grinder."

Mariska nodded. "I looked all over. It isn't here."

"Someone probably liked it and stole it," said Carolina.

Charlotte had eaten her breakfast by the time Declan shuffled into the room, bags beneath his eyes. "Good morning," he mumbled.

"You look like you didn't sleep," said Charlotte.

The side of his mouth flashed the curl of a smile. "Thanks."

"Want some bacon?" asked Carolina. She had a few slices on a spatula and turned to look at Declan. One slid from the utensil and slapped to the floor at her feet.

"Whoops." She dropped the other slices onto a paper towel and bent to pick up the escapee. "I'll eat this one."

"No!" said Declan, lunging forward. He snatched the bacon from her hand, and she stood, stumbling back a step, her mouth agape.

Declan stood holding the bacon, pinched between his fingers.

"What are you doing with that?" asked Carolina once she'd found her feet.

"Uh..."

She scowled. "I told you, *I'll* eat that one. I wasn't going to give it to *you*."

"Uh..." Declan raised the bacon to his mouth and, grimacing, stalled. He looked to Charlotte as if searching for help.

"Now *you're* going to eat it?" Carolina asked, looking at him as if he'd grown a second head.

"Um..."

Abby padded into the kitchen, her nose twitching at the meaty smells.

Declan glanced at the dog. "Sure. I'm going to eat— *whoops*." He bobbled the bacon until it flew out of reach and fell at the soft-coated Wheaten's feet.

Abby glanced at the bacon and then back at Declan, like a child asking for permission to tear into her Christmas gifts. Her body quivered with the strain of being a good girl.

"Don't let her eat that," said Charlotte.

"No problem. Here Abby..." Declan moved like molasses toward the fallen strip of meat. He bent at the knees, and

Charlotte thought she heard him whisper something to the dog.

Abby scooped the bacon into her mouth and gobbled it down.

"Oh shoot," said Declan. He stood and shrugged. "She was too fast for me."

Charlotte frowned.

Something's up.

She stood and took her plate to the sink. "Hey, Dec, could you help me with the ladder in our room? I can't get the thing to fold."

"That is if you're done juggling bacon," added Carolina, squinting at him.

He offered a nervous chuckle. "Sure. Absolutely. I'll be right back."

"Can't wait," said Carolina.

Charlotte and Declan moved together toward the stairs, and she urged him out of the room. It was clear to her that Carolina suspected something was up, and she didn't want to give her a chance to inquire *what.*

Prodded by Charlotte, Declan hustled upstairs to her room, and she closed the door.

"You can tell me what that was all about now," she said.

He sighed. "Seamus was up last night. I found him in the kitchen. He made a UV light."

"He *made* a UV light?"

Declan nodded. "Out of tape and a blue permanent marker. It was pretty amazing, really."

"Why?"

"Because I didn't think you could make an ultra-violet light. I thought they had special bulbs or—"

"Not *why was it amazing.* Why did he make it?"

"Oh. To look for blood splatter. All that talk about how the neighbors might be using this house to dismember bodies was keeping him awake."

"Did he find anything?"

"Blood smears and blood mist. Couple splatters in odd places that a person wouldn't think to clean."

Charlotte nodded. "I get it now. The bacon fell on the *blood floor*."

Declan nodded. "I couldn't let Carolina eat bacon that had fallen on invisible blood splatter."

"Agreed. *Yuck.* And you couldn't bring yourself to eat it either—hey, wait a second—you fed that to my *dog*."

"Sorry."

Charlotte's lip curled. "Remind me not to kiss her for a while."

"And if you do, give me a heads up," said Declan.

Charlotte sat on the edge of the bed, mulling over the new information. "We need to see that freezer."

"What freezer?"

"The one next door. When I asked if they had free space for our meat, Emmitt mentioned a freezer, and then Dinah said it was broken. She acted very squirrely about it, though."

"Funny you should mention squirrels. Seamus chased one last night."

"Where? Downstairs?"

"Yep. He thinks it had something in his little paws too. It shot out the hole in the wall before he could grab it."

Charlotte snorted. "Good thing. I suspect grabbing squirrels never turns out the way you hope."

"That's what he said. Anyway, he followed it outside, but it disappeared near another hole leading to the Elder-Care-o-lina's lower level. Maybe they are keeping a body in their freezer?"

"Maybe, but now that I think about it, squirrels couldn't get into a freezer. Maybe Dinah's strange reaction was less about the freezer and more about the lower level in general."

Declan nodded. "Right. Maybe it's just stuffed down there somewhere, and she didn't want you near the freezer for fear you'd see the body."

Charlotte turned to look at the clock on the bedside table. "Where is Seamus? Is he still sleeping?"

Declan shrugged. "Probably. He was up half the night."

Charlotte stood. "Go wake him up. I need him to romance the nurse into letting him see the lower level."

"Later," said Seamus, pushing open the door.

Charlotte and Declan turned to face him.

"Were you out there eavesdropping the whole time?" asked Declan.

"Aye. Good thing, too. You were in here talking about *me*."

"What do you mean *later*?" asked Charlotte.

Seamus rubbed his head and yawned. "My back is killing me, and I need a plan. And *bacon*."

He turned and shuffled down the hall.

CHAPTER TWENTY

Bob and Chuck enjoyed their afternoon bourbon at three-thirty. It had been a long day of touching up paint and fixing hinges, and they deserved a break—for at least as long as Mariska and Carolina were taking showers and were unable to *stop* them.

"—it's too much. I can't work my charms on her any more or—" Seamus cut short his comment as he and Declan entered the great room. He stared at Bob and Chuck, seeming surprised to see them.

"Who ya seducin'?" asked Chuck.

Seamus and Declan looked at each other.

"You two and Charlotte have been up to something since we got here. Tell us what's up or no bourbon for you," said Bob.

Seamus grimaced and patted Declan on the arm. "Well, there you go. They've left us no choice." He retrieved two glasses from the kitchen cabinets and sat.

Bob poured the newcomers two fingers of bourbon as Seamus shared their desire to check the lower level of the Elder Care-o-lina for bodies.

"You really think there's a body down there?" asked Bob.

Seamus shrugged. "Only one way to find out."

Chuck slowly twirled his glass in his hand. "You know, the weather around here isn't great, but there's never a dull moment. The last time we had dead bodies back home, it was water skiers in a propeller, down at the lake." Chuck glanced at the butter dish, still tucked at the end of the kitchen counter. "Come to think of it, it's not *that* much different."

"I'll do it," said Bob. He looked at Chuck and pointed to him with his thumb. "*We'll* do it."

"Do what?" asked Declan.

"We'll investigate the freezer angle."

Seamus scowled. "How are you two going to get in there?"

Bob didn't skip a beat. "I'm going to pretend I need to inspect their HVAC system. I'll tell them I'm working on ours, and I need to compare."

Seamus stroked his chin. "That's actually not bad. How'd you come up with that?"

"It's true. I *was* working on our HVAC, and I did almost go over there. Decided to have a bourbon instead when I heard Mariska and Carolina say they were going to get cleaned up for dinner."

"So you know how to work on HVAC systems? You can sound like you know what you're doing?"

Bob scoffed. "Sure."

"I don't know. It might be dangerous," said Declan.

Seamus tucked back his chin. "But if *I* end up locked in a freezer, you're okay with that?"

Declan took a sip of his bourbon. "Sneaking around is what you *do*. Anyhow, if you end up in a freezer, I figure you got off easy."

"You might be right there. But Bob has a good plan—"

Declan shook his head. "But who knows what those people are capable of or who they really are? If Bob and Chuck—"

"They're talking about us like we aren't here," interrupted Chuck.

"I noticed that." He rested his forearms on his thighs and leaned forward. "I'll be *fine*. Chuck's coming with me. He's a black belt. Any funny business and *hi-yah!*" Bob slashed at the air with his hand.

Chuck nodded. "I am. It's true. Hi-yah."

Declan scowled at the two older men. "How much have you guys had to drink?"

Bob grinned. "Enough to think this sounds like a lot of fun." He and Chuck high-fived.

Seamus scratched his jaw. "What the heck. What could go wrong?"

Declan sighed.

Seamus spent the next fifteen minutes walking Bob and Chuck through what to look for, what to do and what *not* to do.

Bob stood and finished his glass. "Consider it done."

Chuck rose and followed suit, down to echoing Bob's words. "Consider it done."

Chuck marched to the kitchen to put on his boots and jacket while Bob donned the spare set.

"We should probably take a roadie. Might be the last chance we get for a while," said Chuck as his hand settled on the doorknob to head outside. He made an about-face, grabbed his glass from the kitchen counter, and filled it with bourbon just short of the lip.

"You didn't get mine?" asked Bob as Chuck returned to his side.

"We'll share," said Chuck.

Bob clinked an imaginary glass to Chuck's real one and, with a final wave at Seamus and Declan, headed outside.

The rain had eased, and though it was nearing evening, the sky was the brightest it had been all day. The two men sloshed across the yard and up the front steps of the Elder Care-o-lina to ring the bell.

A woman dressed in a white nurse's uniform answered the door.

"Can I help you?" she asked.

"I've had dreams that started this way," mumbled Chuck. Bob elbowed him.

"Oof!" Chuck scrambled to keep his glass from sloshing.

Bob smiled at the nurse. "Hello, my good lady. We're from next door. My name's Bob, and this is Chuck."

"Hi," croaked Chuck.

"Julie," said the nurse.

"We're working on the furnace next door, and we need a frame of reference A quick peek at a working unit. Since your house seems to have been built in the same style and around the same time as ours, we suspect it had the same builder. We wanted to take a peek at your system and see if the sticker that wore off of ours is still there."

Julie scowled. "I don't know. Emmitt is taking a nap—"

"It will be *two* seconds, and then we'll be out of your hair. What if I promise to leave our muddy boots on the porch?" said Bob.

Julie sighed. "Fine, I guess. Just hurry."

The men stepped out of their boots and walked inside.

"Go around the stairs and then go down," said Julie, pointing.

"Yep. It's just like our house," said Chuck.

They walked downstairs and flipped on the light. The big room was largely empty. Whereas someone had put a sofa, some rugs, and a workbench on their lower level, the nursing home used the space solely as a storage area. Boxes lined one wall.

Chuck elbowed Bob in the ribs. "There's the freezer."

Bob followed Chuck's pointing finger to a large white box in the corner.

"It's running, but it has a padlock," said Chuck. He walked

to the freezer and flipped the lock, so it clattered back into place.

"Why would you padlock a freezer?" asked Bob.

"To keep the bodies from crawling out?"

Bob grimaced. "I think that proves it. We gotta go tell Seamus."

Chuck nodded, his gaze drifting back to the freezer. "Should we try and pry it open?"

Bob considered this. It seemed like a lot of work.

"Nah. We'll let the cops do that." He wandered to the water heater and read the label on the side of the tank while Chuck looked around for bodies.

"See anything?" asked Bob when he was done.

"Nah. Nothing but boxes of junk."

"Okay. I got what I needed. Let's go."

"Did you boys find what you need?" called a voice from the top of the stairs.

Bob motioned to Chuck, and the two of them tromped back to the main floor.

"Thank you. That was perfect," said Bob as he reached the landing.

Chuck held up his half-empty glass in salute.

Julie walked ahead of them to open the front door and usher them away. With a last doff of invisible caps, the men walked into their boots and down the outside stairs.

Bob paused on the patio beneath the back stairs of their house. "Let's finish the drink before we go back in."

"Out here?" asked Chuck, tucking back against the house to avoid the light rain.

He nodded. "I'm only allowed to drink on Bourbon Club nights and vacations. If Mariska catches me with a drink this early, she'll shut me down for my evening cocktail. Maybe the rest of the vacation. I'm allowed to enjoy a cocktail—I'm just not allowed to *look* like I'm enjoying a cocktail."

Chuck nodded. "I know *exactly* what you mean. I'm under similar restrictions."

"Sisters."

They rolled their eyes in unison and then passed the pour back and forth, taking turns sipping.

Bob stared at the yard as Chuck took his turn. A thin sheet of water covered everything in sight. Catching a flash of movement, he spotted a ghost crab scuttling through the slop.

What looked like an eyeball was stuck to the tip of his claw. The orb watched Bob as the crab scuttled by.

Bob remained mesmerized until the crab disappeared around the side of the house.

He glanced at Chuck. His friend stared at the same spot where the crab had disappeared.

"Did you see what I saw?" asked Bob.

Chuck nodded. "Yup."

Bob sighed. "You know, if we told everyone we saw something crazy out here—"

"The wives wouldn't let us drink for the rest of the year," said Chuck, finishing his thought.

"So that being said, did we just see—"

"Nope." Chuck handed him the glass with a splash left inside.

Bob finished the last swig and headed for the stairs.

"I didn't think so."

CHAPTER TWENTY-ONE

Seamus lay on the ground armed with his flashlight, peering beneath the neighbor's outdoor shower and into the hole where the squirrel had disappeared. Creeping on his hands and knees like an army man, his face hovered inches from the gap. He raised his flashlight.

The beam illuminated a man's face, staring back at him through the ragged hole. Milky eyes locked on him. Seamus yelped and scrambled back, only to find himself pinned beneath the walls of the shower. The milky-eyed man's hand reached through the hole, his long, boney fingers clawing at his shirt—

Seamus awoke in a pool of sweat.

He glanced at the clock.

Three thirty-three.

Outside he could hear the wind still roaring. The pounding of rain had stopped. He left his bed and threw on khaki shorts and a t-shirt before heading downstairs.

Seamus shuffled to the sliding glass door of their vacation home and stared outside, unable to see much more than a light rain crossing the path of the porch light.

The storm had eased. That was good.

He turned and found himself staring through the side

window that overlooked the Elder Care-o-lina.

The window that overlooked their outdoor shower.

He shivered, recalling his dream.

In his mind's eye, he pictured the squirrel disappearing through the hole behind the outdoor shower.

Was the creature running to hide more bits or get more?

At the time, he'd been half-joking with himself, but the more he thought about a body hiding in the neighbor's lower level, the more it made sense. It would be impractical to try and bury a body in the seashore's shifting sands. And a storm could create a logistical problem, one that meant keeping the body at home longer than they'd planned...

Bob had said the Elder Care-o-lina's freezer was humming along and padlocked. Dinah had told him the freezer was broken.

There was little reason to lock a freezer and even less reason to lock a broken one.

Of course, there were the *squirrels*. They were an argument *against* the body being in the freezer. Unless somehow they'd dug a hole into that, too.

Maybe there were multiple bodies.

Maybe the squirrels were picking from a buried body, and a *new* body sat in the freezer awaiting burial.

Frustrated, Seamus plodded up the stairs to his bed, where he spent some time staring at the ceiling.

It went against everything in his nature to sit around and *wait* for the tide to recede so they could call the police and start searching for bodies. Back in Miami, he'd seen the "proper channels" in action too many times. People called the police, the police waited for warrants, and by the time the warrants were procured, the evidence was gone, and so were the bad people.

That's how he'd made his money in Miami. He was the "back channel." He could do things the cops couldn't do—in the interest of justice—and the cops trusted him to keep his mouth shut.

Of course, the cops usually had good reason for circumventing the rules. He didn't have any actual evidence of wrongdoing at the Elder Care-o-lina, other than the criminal act of watching sappy movies.

Maybe the medical records Charlotte found were sufficient proof. Maybe not proof of a *body*, but proof that they were hiding *something.*

Seamus glanced at the glowing red numbers on his bedside clock.

Four-fifteen.

It would be daybreak soon.

Maybe I can slip in where the animals come and go.

Seamus sat up and patted his belly.

Maybe.

It wouldn't hurt to look.

Once again, he padded down the stairs and slipped into the spare jacket.

Abby appeared in the kitchen, staring at him.

He raised his finger to his lips as he opened the door.

"Sssh."

The dog watched him leave.

Outside, he raised his face to the sky. The rain had stopped. A strong breeze ruffled his hair.

Walking with his head down, hands thrust in his pockets, Seamus crossed the yard and tucked himself inside the Elder Care-o-lina's outdoor shower.

It was a luxury to have walls surrounding his chosen break-in location.

He jerked the thin sheet of wood that covered the side of the house. It shifted enough for him to confirm it masked a large hole where a window had once been. Someone had nailed wood over it to cover the hole, but the corner had come loose.

With a little additional gnawing, the cats had been able to use it as an escape hatch.

Or the squirrels had created a place of entry. He wasn't sure which now.

Seamus tugged at the wood, but its position behind the shower made it too awkward to pry. Working at it, he managed to pop a nail from the upper half and slide away the board.

He'd started to sweat, but at least he hadn't had to *gnaw* it away.

Score one for opposable thumbs.

Seamus stuck his head inside the lower level of the Elder Care-o-lina and found it too dark to see. He debated whether to tumble in head first or feet first.

He made a decision.

Feet.

Laying on his stomach, he shimmied his legs through the hole until he'd entered to the waist. His toe hit something, and he tapped around, attempting to judge the size and sturdiness of the object beneath him.

It felt like the chest freezer Bob had described to him.

He rested half his weight on it. It held. Bracing himself with his hands, he lowered his remaining weight.

It still held.

Seamus smiled.

He slid the rest of the way into the room.

Though both houses had large flood lights, little of that illumination made it through the hole he'd created. Seamus climbed down from the freezer and shuffled toward where he imagined the stairs would be. After some trial and error, he found the light switch and turned it on.

Seamus scanned the room.

Yep, he'd landed on the freezer.

A combination lock hung from the top loading door of the

freezer, slipped through a metal latch.

Seamus sighed. It had been a while since he'd cracked a combination lock, and the process involved a fair amount of math. The trick was to pull and turn the lock until he could find the sticking points. The first number would lie between those two points. By the third number, there were more possibilities—and more math—involved.

In his heyday, he'd been able to crack a combination lock in about fifteen minutes. Now, both his fingers and his math skills threatened to fail.

Seamus spotted a hammer lying on a wooden shelf unit against the wall.

That would be faster.

Seamus slipped the claw of the hammer behind the metal clasp that held the lock and pried as quietly and steadily as he could until he felt a *pop!*

He moved to the other side of the lock plate and pried again. This side released much more quickly. The sudden release of the plate caused the hammer to fly from his hand. It hit the wall with some force before ricocheting back and striking him on the side of the head.

The lock clattered to the ground as Seamus slapped a hand over his mouth to keep from yelping.

Grimacing, he froze, listening for noises upstairs.

It appeared the residents were all deep sleepers.

Seamus stood in front of the freezer and, taking a moment to brace himself, lifted the lid.

"What the..."

"Freeze!" shouted a voice.

It sounded close.

A second after Seamus heeded the command, he heard the sound of someone pumping a shotgun.

CHAPTER TWENTY-TWO

"You're up early," said Charlotte as Declan hit the bottom of the stairs. She perched the kitchen table in her newly adopted *usual spot* with a cup of coffee. Even without the wafting smell of bacon, she'd been unable to sleep in. She attributed that to the body parts and blood splatter accumulating around her as she slept.

"I heard you making coffee. I'm surprised the others aren't up yet. That bean grinder sounds like you're grinding down a stump."

"You know Mariska and her fresh coffee. Thank goodness for the portable bean grinder, or we'd never get her to vacation anywhere."

Declan poured himself a cup. "Any sign of the others yet?"

"No. I think all this maintenance work is starting to catch up to the older crowd. I know it's starting to catch up with me."

"You should have slept in."

Charlotte sighed. "Tried. Failed. I wanted to look at that lettering on the flesh blob again. It's really hard to tell—it *could* be a piece of Mr. Marino's tattoo or not."

"That covers all the possibilities."

"Exactly."

Declan sat. "Let's pretend it *is* Mr. Marino in the butter dish. What then?"

"Then we'd have to assume Emmitt or Dinah or Emmitt *and* Dinah had something to do with it. They're in charge. Oh, and maybe James, the missing owner."

"Maybe he's more than missing."

Charlotte nodded. "Right. Maybe *he's* the body. Maybe he found out about Mr. Marino and threatened to go to the police."

Declan took a sip. "Maybe we have bits of both. Mr. Marino, James, and who knows who else."

"If you could get away with it again and again, who knows how many people you might knock off and then pretend to house?"

"Could be a *lot* of bodies."

"A *lot*. More than can fit in a freezer."

They fell silent, considering the number of bodies that might be piling up at the Elder Care-o-lina.

"What would they *do* with that many hypothetical bodies?" asked Declan.

"That's what I'm wondering. Having them properly buried would not only be expensive but would also start a paperwork trail. The veteran benefits agency would stop sending checks."

"So if they grew the scam, they'd have a body problem."

"The squirrels don't seem to find it a problem. Maybe that's the plan: let the squirrels distribute the bodies all over the island a little bit at a time."

"They'd definitely have to come up with a plan for the remains before they started killing people on a regular basis."

Charlotte nodded. "You'd think. It's not like this was a crime of passion."

"I hope not. Ick."

"Unless...what if he just *died*?"

"Of natural causes?"

"Yes. And it occurred to them that they'd *really* like to keep receiving his checks?"

Declan twisted his lips into a knot, seemingly mulling her suggestion. "That seems like the most likely scenario, doesn't it? It moves them down a notch from *evil, calculating monsters* to *greedy, opportunistic monsters.*"

"Maybe James didn't agree and—"

A loud *boom!* reverberated through the room, and Charlotte dropped her thought. Coffee sloshed onto Declan's sweatpants as he jumped.

"That wasn't thunder," said Charlotte.

"That sounded like a *gunshot*," agreed Declan.

They stood and moved to the front windows, scanning the yard and beach, illuminated by the dim light of the rising sun.

"I don't see anything," said Charlotte.

She heard another bang come from the direction of the back door and turned to find Declan gone.

"Declan?"

There was no answer.

Caught by a breeze, the back door slapped against the wall, and she hurried to it. From there, she could see Declan already on the ground and running over the dunes.

"Declan!" she screamed into the wind.

He kept running.

She traced his most evident path forward and spotted another man on what remained of the beach, running toward the ocean. He weaved left and right, stumbling across the sand. The man's stocky build felt familiar to her.

Seamus?

Reaching the water's edge, the man splashed into the

ocean, waves crashing around him as he fought to break through. A third figure stood on the beach behind him, holding what looked like a long gun.

She watched as the armed man's attention left the man in the water and moved to Declan.

"Declan—he's got a gun!" she screamed, though she knew he couldn't hear. The wind blew off the water. Any words sent in that direction tumbled right back to her.

The man with the gun looked in her direction and lowered his weapon. He bolted back toward the dunes and the Elder Care-o-lina. She recognized him from his large frame and the lumbering way he moved.

Emmitt.

She turned back to Declan, who had lost any interest he might have had in Emmitt. He ran into the water after Seamus, who had reached deep water and was moving quickly down the beach.

Too quickly.

He must be caught in a riptide.

Declan raced down the beach to get ahead of Seamus. Charlotte felt helpless. Even if she was a great swimmer—which she wasn't—she was much too far behind to be of any assistance.

She silently prayed for Declan and Seamus and was determined to do *something*. She ran down the stairs, hoping to catch the gunman off-guard. If it was Emmitt, as she suspected, she hoped he would talk to her. At the very least, she had to try and *distract* him. She didn't want him shooting Declan and Seamus the moment they left the water.

If they left the water...

Charlotte shook her head, refusing to entertain the thought.

Charlotte searched the area for a makeshift weapon as she ran toward Emmitt's yard. She grabbed the lid from a metal trashcan for a shield and scooped up a gardening shovel as her sword. She didn't think the lid would stop a bullet, but it made her feel better to think she might slow one down.

She reached the backyard of the Elder Care-o-lina at the same time as Emmitt.

"Stop!" she screamed.

He stopped and looked at her, the hand holding the gun raising.

Uh oh.

Charlotte dove to the patchwork of beach and dune grass that separated their yards, sand blasting into her mouth as she tried to catch herself. Her hand slid through the wet grit as she face-planted into the sand. She gagged and spat.

Hearing no gunshot, she pushed to a low crouch and searched for Emmitt. She spotted him heading for the far side of the building.

Still sputtering, she leapt to her feet. A moment before Emmitt would have disappeared to the opposite side of the house, a naked foot appeared at Emmitt's eye level.

It struck him in the face. *Hard.*

She paused and watched as Emmitt's head snapped back with the force of the blow. She couldn't be sure in the dim light, but she *thought* she saw *teeth* fly off.

The gun spun from Emmitt's hand as he tumbled backward. Charlotte broke into a sprint, hoping to secure the gun before he could recover from the blow.

As she neared the weapon, Chuck stepped out from the side of the building, reaching for the gun at the same time she lunged for it.

"Chuck! What the—"

Seeing she had the shotgun, Chuck moved to position himself between her and Emmitt's unmoving body.

"I saw the whole thing. Went around the front of the house to cut him off," said Chuck.

She looked at Emmitt. Blood trickled from the side of his mouth. "What did you do to him?"

Chuck grinned. "I side-kicked him in the face."

"I'll say."

Charlotte's arms felt jittery, adrenalin coursing through her veins.

"Why don't you hand me that," said Chuck, reaching for the gun.

She handed it to him and turned to face the beach.

Declan.

"Declan swam out to save Seamus."

Chuck scowled. "They're swimming?"

Charlotte bolted for the beach.

CHAPTER TWENTY-THREE

Declan yelled at his uncle, but it didn't take long to realize there had to be a good reason for Seamus to be splashing into the frigid North Carolina ocean. That's when he saw the man with the gun.

"Stop!" he barked at the man.

At the sound of his voice, the gunman's head turned, his arm swinging in tandem.

Oops.

That's when it occurred to Declan that screaming at armed men wasn't the *smartest* thing to do. As planned, he'd distracted the gunman from his uncle, but as the man turned his weapon towards him—

Declan dropped to the sand.

No gunshot rang out.

Crouched like a cat, he watched the gunman turn and hasten toward the Elder Care-o-lina. A thought occurred to him.

That looks like Emmitt.

Declan didn't have time to wonder why Emmitt was trying to kill Seamus. He leapt back to his feet and sprinted down the shoreline. In the water, Seamus was swimming now, his body sweeping down the beach almost faster than Declan could keep pace on land.

His uncle had been snatched by a riptide.

Declan grit his teeth and pressed on, determined to race far enough ahead of his uncle so when he entered the water, the riptide could push Seamus directly into his arms.

Fifty yards ahead, he veered into the ocean, diving through the oncoming surf once he'd reached a safe depth. He broke through a massive wave, duck-diving like a board-less surfer. His head rang with pain. The icy water felt more like a brick wall than a liquid.

Swimming between sets, he dove again as the next wave rose and crashed. After being battered by the surf, he broke through. The seas calmed, and he found himself beyond the breakers.

Declan swam with long powerful strokes. At home he swam daily, but the glacial, frothing seas of North Carolina were *nothing* like his Florida lap pool.   He pushed himself, knowing he had to reach Seamus before the riptide dragged his uncle under, or hypothermia froze his limbs.

While he'd made it past the waves, the ocean still roiled with the force of the passing storm. Salt stung his eyes. Every turn of his head came with life-giving air *and* water clamoring to fill his lungs.

He paused, allowing his legs to fall beneath him as he trod water and scanned the sea. He had to confirm Seamus' location. If he lost sight of his uncle, he knew there would be little chance of finding him again.

He saw a commotion of splashing water fifteen yards away. Seamus whirled toward him, thrashing to stay above water.

"*Float!*" Declan screamed, returning to his breaststroke. He was nearly there.

When he paused a second time, he found Seamus close,

paddling for him. His uncle grabbed him, nearly pulling him under.

"You can't—let me go. It'll kill us both," he sputtered.

Declan wrestled him still. "Stop it...stop fighting me. *Relax.*"

Seamus' thrashing stopped, and they flowed together in the riptide, gliding parallel to the beach. Declan felt his uncle's body go limp.

A snake of red swirled around Seamus' body.

"You're hit?" asked Declan.

Seamus coughed as the churning chop peppered them with spray. "Shoulder."

Declan curled his arm beneath Seamus' and across his barrel chest, pulling him against his own body, keeping the older man's head above water.

He twisted his torso, swimming diagonally toward shore, making slow progress as the riptide fought to pull them further out to sea.

Declan's arms and back throbbed, his lungs aching from the seawater. Nearly spent, he found his speed increasing without extra effort. A forming wave engulfed them, plucking them from the grip of the riptide and tossing them toward shore. Declan let that wave and the next do the work until he could touch the bottom.

"Do you think you can stand?" he asked.

Seamus' lips were blue, his teeth chattering so violently he could barely speak. "Like nothing better."

Finding his feet, Seamus shuffled forward through the shallow water, Declan guiding him as he fought his own exhaustion.

Shallows weren't good enough. Dry land wasn't good enough. They had to make it inside, or they would escape drowning only to die from the cold.

"Sh...sh...shooter," warned Seamus.

Declan scanned the shoreline.

"One thing at a time," he said.

Charlotte appeared, waving with both hands high above her head as she ran toward them.

CHAPTER TWENTY-FOUR

Everyone gathered in the great room to stare at the still-unconscious Emmitt. He lay on the sofa, his wrists and ankles zip-tied.

Seamus' shoulder wound had turned out to be more of a massive abrasion than a hole caused by the close, but indirect, contact of a shotgun blast. It looked terrible, but Charlotte pointed out it was better than a trench through his skull.

The beach was still too swamped for cars to traverse, so there would be no trip to the hospital for the Irishman. Darla and Mariska played nurse, fawning over the wound, while Caroline barked instructions. Unable to find proper medical supplies, they'd rinsed out the mottled mess with vodka and cut a kitchen towel into a makeshift bandage secured with duct tape.

"Bandage looks worse than the wound," said Seamus, his lips still tinged with blue. The ladies had insisted on inspecting his wounds before they'd let him take a warming shower.

"If you have a better idea, let us know," said Darla.

Declan entered the room, toweling his hair after taking his shower to warm his core. "He's still out?" he asked upon spotting Emmitt.

Charlotte nodded. "Chuck got him good."

Chuck grinned.

Wound bandaged, Seamus donned the dry sweatshirt Charlotte had fetched for him and leaned in to lightly slap Emmitt's cheek.

"Hey, *you*, wake up. Let's go."

Emmitt's eyes fluttered open, and he jerked away from Seamus. He struggled to sit, an expression of both agitation and fear on his face.

"What's going on? What is this?" he asked.

Seamus helped Emmitt right himself into a sitting position and then pushed him back down as he tried to rise to his feet.

"You shot me," said Seamus, pulling out the collar of his sweatshirt and pointing to his kitchen towel bandage.

Emmitt gaped and froze that way, seemingly giving himself a moment to recall the details that led to his current predicament. "*You* tried to attack me," he said after a measured pause.

Seamus leaned forward and stuck a finger in Emmitt's face. "Why wouldn't I? You were holding a gun on me."

"You'd broken into my house!"

Seamus shut his mouth and straightened, scratching at his head with his good arm. "He's got a point there."

"What were you doing at his house?" asked Darla.

"Take it from the top," suggested Charlotte.

Seamus looked at the others, all of whom stared at him as if *he* were the one who needed to explain his actions.

I'm the one who was shot.

He sighed. "Fine. I woke up too early, and I couldn't stop thinking about the squirrels and the body parts—"

"Body parts!" exclaimed Emmitt. "Who are you people?" He tried again to stand, and Seamus put two fingers on his forehead to push him back down.

"Calm down."

Emmitt remained still but for his gaze, which bounced from person to person as if he thought any one of them might attack him at any moment.

"Keep going," said Declan.

Seamus continued. "I wanted to find out if they were hiding a body in their basement and—"

Emmitt tried to protest again and was silenced by Seamus' glare. He pressed his lips together and scowled back at Seamus as the Irishman continued.

"As I was *saying*, thanks to the squirrel, I knew their lower level wall had a hole. Turns out it was a big hole, so I slipped through it and pried the lock off the freezer."

"Was there something in it?" asked Mariska, visibly tensing with excitement.

Seamus nodded. "*Meat*. Turkey, some steaks, two giant tubs of vanilla ice cream—" He looked at Emmitt. "Can't you get something more interesting than vanilla?"

Emmitt squinted at him. "Why would you think there was a *body* in our freezer?"

"Why do you keep it locked?" snapped Seamus, sounding very much like the lawyers he admired on television.

Emmitt appeared unimpressed by his cross-examination, scoffing to make his disdain for Seamus' logic known. "We have *dementia patients*. They wander off and do odd things. We keep it locked for their safety."

"Seems pretty reasonable when he puts it that way," said Declan.

"Why did Dinah say the freezer was broken?" asked Charlotte.

Seamus held up a finger. "Yeah, why?"

Emmitt rolled his eyes. "Because it *is* broken. It's too cold, and we can't seem to turn it down. If you'd really *looked* at the food in there, you would have seen it's all frostbitten."

"Oh. I must have missed that. I was a little busy staring at your *shotgun*," said Seamus.

Emmitt set his jaw. "Look, I was protecting the house. I never had any intention of shooting you. But then you tried to wrestle the gun—"

Seamus grunted.

"But you chased him down the beach with the gun," said Charlotte.

"I wasn't chasing him to *shoot* him. I was just chasing him. I didn't know what else to do."

Charlotte walked away from the group and returned with the butter dish. She placed it on the living room table in front of Emmitt before lifting the lid. Upon registering the contents, he jumped back in his seat.

"Is that an *ear*?"

"Yes. And that's a finger, and that's a blob of flesh."

Emmitt struggled against his bindings. "You people are monsters—"

Seamus slapped the top of Emmitt's head. "Calm down. We found all of these things in the house. Squirrels and possibly your *cats* were bringing them to us like trophies."

Emmitt fell still. "The cats? So they *were* getting out?"

"The hole in the wall, remember?"

"But where would they get *those* things?"

"That's what we wanted to know," said Declan.

"Should I tell him everything?" asked Charlotte.

Seamus crossed his arms against his chest and nodded. "Might as well."

Charlotte took a deep breath and locked eyes with Emmitt. "We think these parts belong to Mr. Marino."

Emmitt's eyes grew wide. "Mr. *Marino*?" Why—"

Charlotte continued. "We know you're pretending to care for him, but that he's more than likely dead. There's no point in denying it."

Emmitt sat back, appearing defeated. He took a deep

breath.

"He is dead," he mumbled.

"So you admit you're keeping his benefits?"

Emmitt nodded.

"Where's he buried?"

Emmitt's brow knit. "What?"

"Where did you hide the body?" asked Seamus.

"We didn't *hide* the body. He's buried in the cemetery." Emmitt's eyes began to water. "We didn't mean to do it. I mean, we didn't do it on *purpose*."

"You didn't kill him?"

"No, we didn't kill him! His checks just kept coming. They forgot to file the paperwork, and we didn't go out of our way to correct the error."

"But then, who is *this*?" asked Charlotte, pointing to the body bits in the butter tray.

Emmitt shook his head. "I have no idea."

Charlotte flopped into the only remaining empty chair. "That means we're not any farther along on this mystery than we were when we found the finger."

Seamus leaned in to pull his face close to Emmitt's. "Where's James?"

Emmitt frowned. "Last I heard, with his mother in Florida."

Seamus straightened. "Really? Can you prove it?"

"*No.* I wake up one day to find he's gone, and all I have to show for a five-year relationship is a note saying he's moved to Florida."

"Did he say *relationship*?" asked Carolina.

Darla leaned over and whispered something in her ear, and Carolina's eyes widened. "Oh."

"Did you have a falling out over Marino?" asked Seamus.

"No. Keeping the checks *was* his idea. He was *so* excited about it. I was surprised when he left because I had finally relented and agreed *not* to report Marino's death, just to keep him happy."

"So that's why Dinah seemed so weird about James? Because he left you?" asked Charlotte.

Emmitt nodded. "She's furious at him for breaking my heart. She won't even let me say his name."

"What's the timeline here? When did Marino die, and when did James leave?"

"Marino died four months ago. James only left about a week ago."

Charlotte scowled at the butter tray. "Four months? I think these are too fresh to be that old."

"Especially if they weren't kept in a freezer," said Darla.

Seamus found himself locked in a gaze with Charlotte. They were thinking the same thing.

James disappeared a *week* ago.

CHAPTER TWENTY-FIVE

Seamus was about to ask if James had any tattoos when there was a booming crash outside. The *crack!* sounded like an enormous firecracker exploding in the front yard. Everyone jumped, gasping and slapping their hands to their chests.

"What was *that*?" asked Mariska.

The sound had come from the front of the house. With the exception of Emmitt, who remained zip-tied on the sofa, the others scurried toward the foyer. Charlotte reached the knob first and flung open the front door.

The Reptile sat in the middle of the road, its backend pressed against a tree. The pine had toppled and now leaned on a neighboring tree, propped like a drunken friend.

The Reptile's engine revved, pushing the bus deeper into the trunk, wheels kicking sand in all directions.

The group remained on the front porch, too terrified to try their luck crossing the path of the truck.

The wheels stopped whirring. Before anyone could move, *The Reptile* lurched forward and crushed the mailbox in one deft motion.

The snake's eyes glowed and blinked several times before

the truck shuddered into silence. As it did, a giant forked red tongue shot from the front grill, unraveling across the ground as a monstrous hissing noise filled the air.

"Did you know it could do that?" asked Declan.

Seamus shook his head. "No idea."

In the driver's seat, they could see Dinah in a full-blown panic, hands fluttering, and she tried again to start the vehicle.

Seamus stomped down the stairs, muttering.

"For the love of! If she gets that thing started again, she's going to take out the porch and kill us all."

He slammed the driver's side of the bus with the palm of his hand until Dinah opened the window and peered down at him from her perch in the driver's seat.

"What are you *doing*?" he called up to her.

She slammed the window shut again. They heard the bus groan as she tried to shift into gear once more.

"Be careful—she's gonna flatten you like a bug!" screamed Darla.

Seamus searched the porch for help that wasn't coming. Everyone stared back at him, helpless, including the dogs, whose faces he could see peering from the windows. Even Darla's little hot dog was there, her face appearing every few seconds, ears flapping out, as she leapt up to snatch a peek at what the taller dogs could see standing still.

Seamus took a deep breath and bolted in front of *The Reptile* to get to the doors on the opposite side. The truck lurched again as he crossed its path, and the group on the porch all gasped in unison. Luckily, the engine shuddered out once more without moving the truck an inch from where it nestled on the mailbox.

Seamus resumed his banging on the opposite side of the bus.

"Open the door, dammit!" he screamed again.

"You killed Emmitt!" Dinah yelled back at him, wild-eyed.

Seamus stopped banging and took a moment to compose himself. "We did not kill Emmitt."

Dinah started the truck once more. "I saw you. That man kicked him dead, and then you carried him into your house, and I found his toe in the living room."

"His toe?" Seamus jumped as the truck shifted into reverse and blasted back into the trees. This time, the rear end wedged between two pines before the engine died.

Seamus tilted his head back and stared at the sky. "Go get Emmitt," he said to no one in particular, but loud enough for all to hear.

"Why?" asked Darla.

"She thinks we killed him. Go get him."

Declan, Bob, and Chuck went inside and returned with Emmitt, his ankles released and hands still bound.

Seamus pointed at him for Dinah. "See? We didn't kill him."

Dinah stared through the front windshield.

"You shot him."

"He shot *me*," said Seamus, pulling his shirt away to show her the bandage.

"Why would he do that?"

Seamus waved a hand at her. "It's a long story."

"Did he give you that big lump on your head?"

Seamus felt the lump on the side of his forehead where the hammer had struck him while trying to pry away the freezer lock.

"Maybe," he said.

She scowled. "What about his toe?"

Seamus motioned to Emmitt and called to the others. "Make him hold up his feet so she can count his toes."

"This is insane," said Carolina.

Declan assisted Emmitt as he held up one leg and then the other.

Dinah gaped. "Then why is there a toe in our house?"

"Come out of the bleedin' bus, and we'll tell you."

Dinah jerked several times on the driver's side window until it opened. She stuck out her head.

"Are you okay, Emmitt?"

Emmitt nodded. "I'm fine."

"They didn't try to kill you?"

"No."

"It's safe for me to come out?"

"Yes."

Dinah pulled in her head and then thrust it through again.

"Are you only saying that because they're holding a gun to you where I can't see?"

Emmitt sighed. "*No.*"

Dinah exited the bus a moment later, giving Seamus as wide a berth as possible.

"You've wrecked *The Reptile*," said Seamus, inspecting the back of the bus.

Dinah positioned herself on the property line between the two houses, twenty feet from the others.

"Let's go inside and get everything cleared up," said Charlotte.

She turned and led the group back inside until only Seamus and Dinah remained outside.

"After you," said Seamus.

Dinah scowled and stomped up the stairs.

CHAPTER TWENTY-SIX

Inside, they freed Emmitt and shared the story of Seamus' break-in, Emmitt's defense of the home, and Chuck's karate skills.

"I knew you were a bunch of lunatics," said Dinah, still appearing unsettled. "And none of that explains the toe. Julia just about fainted."

Charlotte stood to remove the top of the butter dish. Seeing the contents, Dinah yipped and covered her mouth.

"You could have handled that better," said Declan.

"Sorry. I've gotten so used to it." Charlotte put the lid back on the dish, the cut glass obscuring the contents once more.

"Was that an *ear*?" asked Dinah from behind her palm.

Everyone nodded.

"We've been finding body parts since we arrived. We think the squirrels have been bringing them in. Maybe the cats."

Dinah gasped and dropped her hand to her chest. "*My* cats?"

Charlotte nodded. "So you can understand when we suspected Mr. Marino had been killed, we also thought you had a body stashed somewhere."

Dinah's gaze shot to Emmitt.

"They know about Marino," said Emmitt, answering the question before it could be asked.

"It was a paperwork accident that worked in our favor. James bullied Emmitt into keeping the money," said Dinah, her eyebrows tilting to show her concern.

"Don't worry. We're not running to the police with your benefits scam," said Seamus.

"We're not?" asked Carolina.

Seamus fixed a pointed gaze on Emmitt. "You'll make it right. Right?"

Emmitt nodded, petting his swollen nose. The areas beneath his eyes had darkened like thunderclouds moving across his face.

"We're a little more concerned by the body parts than the benefits scam," added Charlotte.

Dinah nodded. "I could see that. Thank you."

"Well, the storm looks about done," said Darla, who had moved to stare through the large sliders that led to the back porch. "I imagine we'll be able to call in the police soon and let *them* take care of everything."

Charlotte grimaced. She hated that they'd been unable to solve the mystery.

Emmitt stood and thrust a hand toward Seamus. "I'm going to head back to the house. You have my word we'll fix the paperwork. I appreciate you giving me the chance to correct our moment of greed."

Seamus stood and shook. "I appreciate you not killing me."

Dinah shook her head, her jaw clenched. "*Greedy*, that's what James was. Always greedy. I warned you." She shook a finger at Emmitt.

He nodded. "I know. You did. You warned me."

"I told you he used to hit on me when I first brought

Momma there. He thought I had more money than I did. But I told him I wasn't falling for his funny business."

Emmitt put a hand on Dinah's shoulder and gently guided her toward the front door. "You know that isn't possible."

"I'm telling you, he was after me. He was *greedy*."

"Okay. Okay."

Emmitt flashed an apologetic smile to the group and then winced when it made his nose move. With a final wave, he closed the door on Dinah's continued protestations.

"I guess it isn't Mr. Marino," said Charlotte after they'd left.

"Are you sure you believe them?" asked Darla.

Charlotte nodded. "You know, I really do."

"Though the cops will want to check with the funeral home, just in case," said Seamus.

Mariska picked up the butter dish and moved it to its place on the kitchen counter.

"Who are you in there?" she asked it.

"It's a dead person, not a pet, Mariska," said Carolina.

"My money says that's James in the dish," said Chuck.

Bob nodded. "We should place bets. I'll take Marino. I think they're lying."

They reached for their wallets, and Carolina clucked her tongue, glancing sidelong at her sister.

"Couple of degenerates we married."

CHAPTER TWENTY-SEVEN

Charlotte suspected the police would be able to reach them by the next day. The ocean had decided to go back to being *ocean* and stop pretending to be a *beach*. Knowing her chance to identify the body and killer slipped farther away with each tide, she spent the remaining day scouring the yard and the beach. She posited that the body had to be out there somewhere, or the animals wouldn't be able to use it as an *all you can drag around* buffet. If she could find more body or even evidence of digging...

She found nothing.

Seamus and the boys spent the bulk of their day extracting *The Reptile* from between the trees and doing their best to minimize the damage. From her bedroom window, Charlotte watched them try and buff a scraped bumper. Cranky and dejected by her failed search, she'd tried to take her mind off the case by packing her clothes. The group had unanimously decided to call the trip off a week early. As soon as the beach was dry enough to drive on, they planned to hit the road.

Not that they had a choice. All their handiwork would soon be wrapped in crime tape.

Declan passed her open door on his way to his room and stopped.

"Driving you crazy, isn't it? That you don't know who the body is or who killed him?" he said, propping himself against the door jamb.

Charlotte turned and smiled. "Absolutely *bonkers*."

Darla sat in bed, sipping her evening coffee and scrolling through her Facebook timeline. She sniggered.

"You people are crazy. We spent this whole time worried about body bits when we should have been trying to enjoy ourselves." She held up her phone for Charlotte to see. "This is what a vacation is supposed to look like."

Charlotte glanced at the screen. Brenda, again, the background tropical.

"Have you been able to reach her?" she asked.

Darla shook her head. "No. She won't even respond to emails about dead people in her house. She is off the grid."

In the photo that Darla held aloft, Phil sat behind Brenda, wearing his familiar smile.

His very familiar smile. Phil only had one expression, and it was "not impressed." He didn't seem to be enjoying the vacation quite as much as his wife.

"Phil always has that same look on his face—"

Charlotte fell quiet as the sound of tiny footfalls scurried above them. All heads tilted back, and they stared at the ceiling.

"Did you hear that?" asked Declan.

"That didn't sound good. It sounded like *rats*," said Darla, clenching her fists against her chest.

They heard more footsteps followed by a growl, a yelp, and what sounded like a tussle between two angry creatures.

"There's some sort of animal *Fight Club* going on in the attic," said Charlotte.

"I don't think this vacation could get worse if it tried,"

said Darla, her chin dropping to her chest.

Declan pivoted back into the hall, still scanning the ceiling. "Here it is," he said.

Charlotte followed to find Declan pulling a cord that hung from the ceiling. "I thought I remembered seeing attic access out here," he said.

"Oh, don't pull that until I get a weapon or *something*," said Charlotte, grabbing his arm.

Declan paused. "Hm. Good point. I need some light, too. I was doing a little night painting the other day. I think I've still got a flashlight in my room."

Releasing the cord, he jogged down the hall and returned with a long red flashlight. "This thing is heavy. It can serve as a weapon and light."

"Perfect. I think I'll still hang a few steps behind you to be safe."

He grabbed the cord once more. "Ready?"

Not really. She winced and nodded.

"Hold on," said Darla, who had been peering around the corner from her room. She shut the door.

"I think she's got the right idea," said Charlotte.

"I know I do! You two are out of your minds!" yelled Darla from behind the protection of her closed door.

With one last glance at Charlotte, Declan pulled the cord. A two-by-three-foot section of the ceiling creaked open to reveal a folded ladder bolted to the opposite side.

They paused, listening for tiny clawed footsteps.

Nothing.

"I don't hear anything," whispered Charlotte.

"Me neither."

"That's a good thing, right?"

Declan sighed. "Yes. Unless it means it's there, crouched, waiting to jump on my face."

Charlotte nodded. "Right. Unless *that*."

Declan reached for the ladder while Charlotte cowered, preparing for something to fly out of the attic.

"Something smells," said Declan, unfolding the ladder.

Charlotte sniffed. "Ooh. You're right. That's *terrible.* Smells like one of them *lost* critter fight club.

"A *while* ago."

Flicking on his flashlight, Declan mounted the ladder and climbed until his eyes were just above the edge, and he could see into the attic.

"Do you see anything?" asked Charlotte.

He raised his arm to shine the beam into the attic.

"Do you see anything?" she repeated.

He backed a step and looked down at her.

"*No.* But I'm also scared to answer you with my face in the attic. It might draw the attention of whatever the heck is up there."

She moved to the ladder. "Sorry. Tell you what—you go. I'll follow you up."

He grimaced and climbed into the attic. Charlotte waited a moment to see if he was attacked and then followed.

She wasn't too proud to use him as a scout.

"It reeks up here," she said, pinching her nose as she joined him in the attic.

"I know."

She looked up and noticed roofing nails hanging from the ceiling. It looked as if they'd entered a medieval torture device. "No matter what happens, don't stand up straight, or you'll be lobotomized."

Declan rubbed the top of his head. "I know. I already got poked when I first stood. It's killing me."

"*Ouch.* You didn't yip or anything."

"I was trying to look tough for you."

"I appreciate that."

"No problem."

Due to the sloping roof on either side, they could only stand on one wide beam in the very center of the room. Even then, Declan had to duck.

Declan shone the light around the small space. On either side of the plank on which they stood, pink strips of insulation sat tucked between the beams. Scattered on those strips was a menagerie of superfluous household items. Lamps, Christmas decorations, miscellaneous lumpy trash bags, and other items light enough not to crash through the drywall beneath the insulation, nested on the fluffy pink stuffing.

Declan shuffled down the length of the plank. "The smell gets worse down here."

"Great." Charlotte followed, using the ceiling to steady herself and trying her best to avoid impaling her palms on the roofing nails.

A small window marked the end of the line. Declan reached it and shone the flashlight down.

"It looks like there's a hole under—"

A flash of movement made them both scream. Charlotte caught a glimpse of a black and gray, ringed tail before Declan backed into her and her weight shifted too far left. She caught herself on a beam, but not before her left foot slipped off the plank and planted into the stuffing.

For a moment, all felt right with the world. Then her foot burst through the drywall below, and she sank like a runaway elevator, one leg plunging down while the other hung up on the plank on which she'd been standing.

Declan grabbed her flailing arm just as her knee disappeared into the room below, stopping her fall. Beneath her, she heard Darla scream.

"Charlotte, why is your leg sticking from the ceiling? Are you all right?"

"I'm fine," Charlotte called, aware that it might be a lie. She hung from Declan's grasp, panting, her nails digging into his flesh.

"Ow," he said.

"I'll fall if you let go."

"I won't let go. I'm going to lift you back up. Ready?"

She nodded.

With a mighty jerk, Declan lifted her back to her feet.

She put her arms around him and clung there a moment, catching her breath.

"That was scary," she said.

"Though I lost you there for a second," said Declan, chuckling.

"What was that? A raccoon?"

He nodded. "Sorry. It jumped right at me, and I backed into you before I could stop myself."

"Charlotte, are you okay?" called Darla.

Charlotte peered down through the hole left by her leg. Darla stared up at her, sputtering and wiping her face as a fine cloud of plaster showered down.

"I'm fine. There was a raccoon, but it's gone."

Darla put her hands on her hips. "So is half the ceiling!"

Seamus' face appeared beside Darla's.

"What are you two doing up there?" he asked.

Charlotte heard Darla explaining to him about the animal noises. Then she returned her attention to Declan.

"Is that what stinks? The raccoons?" she asked.

He'd already started to inch his way back to the end of the plank.

"Probably. Though, it smells *worse* than animals. It smells like—"

Declan swung the beam of his flashlight to the right and froze. Charlotte gasped and slapped her hand on her mouth. She wasn't sure Darla could take any more screaming.

This was going to be tough, though.

Declan's light revealed a human arm reaching from a

dark green contractor's bag. Three fingers had been gnawed away.

Declan swept the beam around, and Charlotte could see two more bags, one torn, one intact. Hanging from the torn one was the edge of a hacksaw and another shiny object.

"That answers where the saw went. I imagine the pliers are in there, too," said Declan.

The thought of how the tools had been used made Charlotte shiver.

"Is that the shiny thing? Pliers?" she asked.

"I don't think so. That looks like a knob or—"

Charlotte realized the shape of the object was familiar. "It's the *salt shaker*. It's the pepper's missing mate."

Declan scowled. "Why would they hide that?"

Charlotte shook her head, her gaze drifting back to the arm thrusting through the other bag. "The real question is, how many bodies are up here?"

"Don't ask me to count. I'm just glad the chilly weather kept the smell and maggots down."

"*Gross*. I'm done with this." Charlotte inched her way back down the beam toward the exit. "I might have to leave the rest of this to the police."

Declan followed. "I might have to sleep on the bus tonight."

"Take a pillow for me."

They climbed down the ladder. Declan folded it and closed the attic trapdoor before Seamus entered the hall.

"We've got raccoons?" asked Seamus.

Declan nodded. "Among other things."

"Rats?"

Declan shook his head, his eyes wide as he tried to telegraph the severity of the problem to Seamus without saying it out loud.

Darla entered the hall with her suitcase. "Thank goodness

I'm already packed. I'll sleep on the sofa if I have to, but you're not getting me back in a room with a hole that leads to raccoon land above my head." She stopped at the top of the stairs and looked back at them. "And something *stinks* in there now."

Darla headed downstairs, and Seamus turned to Declan and Charlotte.

"What's up? Something is clearly *up*."

"There are bags of body parts up there," said Charlotte, thinking of no easy way to break the news.

Seamus' eyes grew wide. "*Bags?*"

"Trash bags full of bodies. That's the smell. The raccoons were tearing through them and dragging pieces outside," said Declan.

"Dinah will be glad to hear there is even more evidence her cats are innocent," said Charlotte.

"You said *bodies*. More than one?" asked Seamus.

"We couldn't tell and didn't stay to figure it out," said Declan.

"We've got to get the cops here if we have to *helicopter* them in now," said Seamus.

Declan headed for the stairs. "I'll go down and get a hunk of plywood to put over that hole. We don't want the raccoons dropping things through there."

"And to keep the whole house from reeking," said Charlotte.

Seamus nodded. "Good point. If the others get a whiff of that stench, they'll be wantin' to know what's going on. We can't have them all panicking while we're stuck here." Seamus retrieved his phone from his pocket. "I'm going to call the police and let them know to get here ASAP. I think if properly motivated, they'll be able to find a way here by tomorrow morning."

"I'd say we've got some pretty good motivation," said Charlotte.

Seamus nodded toward the stairs as he raised the phone to his ear. "I'll help Dec with the repairs. You go downstairs and keep the others from coming up here until we can get the place aired out a bit."

"So *they* get to sleep tight, never knowing there are bags of body parts above their heads."

"Exactly."

Charlotte sighed and headed downstairs.

"Ignorance *is* bliss."

CHAPTER TWENTY-EIGHT

"What was all that commotion?" asked Mariska as Charlotte entered the main living area. "Did I hear Darla say something about raccoons?"

Charlotte spotted Darla's suitcase against the wall. "She didn't tell you?"

"She headed right into the bathroom muttering something about rabies."

Declan came up the stairs with a hunk of plywood in his hand, paused long enough to nod and smile at the group, and then continued to the second level.

"Why did Declan just run by with a giant piece of wood?" asked Carolina, pausing from her potato peeling.

Charlotte realized how smart Declan had been, offering to fetch the wood instead of getting stuck with the job of telling everyone else *half* the story.

"We heard animals in the attic. Declan and I went to investigate—"

"What was the scream?" interrupted Mariska.

"When I slipped, and my foot went through Darla's ceiling."

"What? Are you okay?"

"I'm fine. The raccoon scared us and then skittered outside."

"Raccoons!" Carolina exclaimed, peeler pausing in mid-peel. "This is the vacation from hell."

"But you love being here with all of us," said Mariska.

Carolina grunted as her sister playfully bumped her hip with her own.

Darla entered the great room and headed for the computer. "I'll write Brenda and tell her she's got critters in the attic."

Darla's comment triggered something in Charlotte's brain.

Something hit me right before we heard the raccoons...

She was staring at the countertop, deep in thought, when Mariska touched her cheek. "You look pale. Are you sure you're okay?"

Charlotte snapped to attention and glanced at the nasty scratches on her thigh. "I'm fine. Couple of scratches."

"Talk about pale. Compared to Phil, Brenda looks like a ghost," said Bob, pausing to peek over Darla's shoulder at the computer on his way to the kitchen.

"She's darker than she was, but you're right—Phil looks like he's really been hitting the beach," said Darla.

Charlotte wandered over to look at Darla's Facebook. The photo she'd seen earlier of Brenda and Phil filled the screen as Darla commented beneath it, telling her friend about the raccoon.

"Is beneath a vacation photo really the place to tell her that her house is full of raccoons?" asked Charlotte.

Darla hit enter. "She's not answering her email. Maybe she'll answer that. She's lucky I didn't mention the ear."

The *thing* in Charlotte's brain began to jiggle again, looking for attention.

Brenda. Something about Brenda...

"Can you go to Brenda's other photos?" she asked.

"Sure." Darla navigated to Brenda's personal page, and Charlotte motioned for her to vacate her seat.

Darla stood. "What's up?"

Charlotte sat and enlarged one photo of Brenda and Phil and then another. "These photos..."

"Bunch of showoffs," said Bob shuffling back to his seat.

Charlotte opened a third photo and finished her thought. "The shadows are off. The light on Phil is different from the light on Brenda."

Darla moved in to squint at the screen. "She's closer to the camera."

"Yes, but that isn't it. Did you say she posted vacation photos before?"

"She always does. About six months ago, she had a whole bunch from Mexico."

Charlotte scrolled back through Brenda's timeline until she hit the next bunch of vacation photos. She found one of Phil on the beach alone, probably taken by Brenda. His pose seemed very familiar. She opened it in a new window and then navigated back to the photos from the current vacation.

"*Look,*" said Charlotte, opening photos old and new beside each other.

Darla stared at the screen and then pulled back, looking at Charlotte with an expression of confusion. "Phil looks exactly the same in both photos. It's the same pose, same expression—"

"The clothes, the skin tone—"

"How can that be?"

Charlotte pointed at the photos. "She's taken this old photo of him, plucked him out of it, and inserted him into the new photo."

Darla gaped. "How?"

"Any photo manipulation program would allow someone

to do it. Photoshop, for example."

"Brenda wouldn't know how to do that."

"Maybe not. But she could have hired someone to do it."

"But *why*? Why would she do that?"

Charlotte sat back in the chair, realizing what had been eating at her. "To make it look like Phil is there when he isn't."

Darla rolled her eyes. "But of course, he's there. Why wouldn't he be there?"

Seamus and Declan entered, and Charlotte smiled at how nonchalant they were trying to appear after sealing the tomb above their heads.

"Hey guys, come here."

The men approached and flanked her chair. Seamus leaned down and whispered in her ear.

"The police said they think they can make it here. It's low tide. They should be here in an hour."

She nodded and pointed to the two vacation photos on the screen. "See anything funny here? This is a new photo, and this is one from a few months ago."

Seamus squinted at the screen. "It's the same photo of the guy."

"But in two different backgrounds," agreed Declan.

"That's Phil, our host. *The owner of this house*," said Charlotte.

"That his wife?" asked Seamus, pointing at Brenda.

"Yes. She just posted—"

She gasped.

"What?" asked Seamus, Declan, and Darla in unison.

She pointed at the obscured MARINES tattoo on Phil's tan chest. "Not A-R ARmy. A-R *mARines*."

Seamus straightened. "Oh."

Declan looked at his uncle, his brow knit before his expression released, and his eyes widened. "*Oh*."

"Oh, *what*?" asked Darla. Her eyes popped wide, and she

put her hand over her mouth. "Oh *no*. You don't think—"

She looked at the butter dish.

"How well do you know Brenda and Phil?" asked Charlotte.

Darla shrugged. "I've known Brenda for years. She lived in my neighborhood in Tennessee, but she was married to Jimmy Bowen, the 'King of Cadillacs' then. I only met Phil a couple of times."

"The King of Cadillacs?"

"He owned a few dealerships."

"They divorced?"

Darla shook his head. "He drowned. Fell into the lake and hit his head."

"Hm," grunted Seamus.

"What's going on?" asked Mariska, wandering over to them, drying her hands on a dish towel.

"They think our friend in the butter dish is Phil," said Darla.

"What? Brenda's Phil?" said Mariska, a little too loudly.

The yelp caught Carolina's attention, and she called from her place at the sink. "What are you people yapping about?"

"Charlotte thinks the person in the butter dish is Phil," said Mariska.

Carolina shrugged and went back to peeling.

Charlotte touched Darla's arm. "Brenda is most likely responsible if she's going to these lengths to pretend he's alive when he isn't."

Mariska huffed. "That's ridiculous. Darla wouldn't be friends with a *murderer*."

"You'd be surprised," mumbled Darla.

Darla moved to the butter dish and lifted the lid. "So you're saying all these body bits are Phil?"

Charlotte joined her and pointed to the *AR* on the flesh blob. "I assumed that was the beginning of *ARMY* when it matched Mr. Marino's tattoo, but it's clipped tight on either side. It could easily be the AR in Phil's MARINE tattoo."

Darla's head dropped. "Why would she do this?"

"Money or sex," said Seamus. "It's always one of those two."

"Phil *was* rich," said Darla.

"Like her first husband," added Declan.

Darla sighed. "This is terrible."

"What's terrible is that we just spent a week trapped in a storm fixing up a house for a *Jezebel*," said Carolina, scowling at them from the kitchen.

"I think I know who helped her with the photo doctoring," said Seamus.

Charlotte leapt back to the computer. "Who?"

He pointed to the glass front door of a colorful shop featured in one of Brenda's vacation photos. When Charlotte looked very carefully, she could make out a form reflected in the glass. She could tell that was the person taking the photo.

"I don't know who it is, but Brenda ended up with his photo on her Facebook, so there's a good chance he's with her."

"I know who it is," said Charlotte. She couldn't see the person's face, but the shirt he wore was easier to read. It said *Clemson* in large white letters.

"There was a picture of James in the upstairs hallway next door. He was wearing a Clemson t-shirt in it."

Seamus' brow knit. "James? But I thought he and Emmitt were a thing—" He looked at Darla. "Just how rich *is* Brenda?"

Darla scoffed. "She was *loaded*. Jimmy's family had been rich to start with—the dealerships were just icing on the cake. Then, Phil—he was rich, too."

Seamus looked at Charlotte. "James might have pretended to be something he wasn't for that much money. Dinah said he was greedy."

"And Brenda might have forgotten Phil when someone

that young took an interest in her," said Darla.

"*Jezabel*," said Carolina from the kitchen.

Charlotte snapped. "That explains the key I found, too. Of course, James would have a key to this house."

"And no doubt he's the one who helped her haul Phil to the attic," added Declan.

All eyes turned to him, and he bit his lip.

"Whoops."

"What about the attic?" asked Darla.

Charlotte closed her eyes. "Now you've done it."

CHAPTER TWENTY-NINE

A week earlier.

"I knew it."

Brenda's husband stood at the threshold of the master bedroom in his Outer Banks vacation home, staring at the man and the woman in his bed.

Brenda stared back at him. She could feel her jaw hanging slack with surprise, so she shut it and instead raised her chin in defiance.

"Are you so shocked? That's *rich*," she said.

He laughed and motioned in the direction of her lover. "Look at him. What is he? Twenty years younger than you?"

"Your mistresses are younger than *that*."

Phil chuckled. "The difference is I *know* they're after my money. You think *he* loves you."

Brenda looked at the man beside her in bed. James smiled and took her hand in his.

"I *do* love her," he said to Phil.

Silently, Brenda groaned. Even she didn't buy James' romantic declaration.

Why was everyone making her fantasy so hard to maintain?

Phil laughed louder.

Brenda pulled her hand from James' and glowered at her husband. "What are you doing here anyway?"

"I came to end this for you before he bleeds us dry."

"I'm not in it for the money—" began James.

"Shut it before my lawyers make your life a living hell, one way or the other."

James swallowed.

Phil turned his attention back to Brenda. "I want him out of my house."

He left before she could respond.

Brenda sat, stunned. Downstairs she could hear Phil dropping ice cubes into a glass, making himself a scotch as if nothing had happened.

"You should divorce him," muttered James.

"Pre-nup."

"What?"

"Pre-nup. If I divorce him, I'll lose everything, and he knows it."

"Will he divorce *you*?"

"I don't know." She turned to James. "But if he did—or if *I* did—we could be together. Wouldn't it be wonderful not to sneak around anymore?"

"Yes." James smiled and squeezed her hand. She could feel the hesitation in his touch. See the disappointment in his eyes.

I'm an old fool.

She knew James didn't love her. Hell—she was pretty sure he was gay.

In her experience, straight men his age didn't stay in such amazing shape.

No. He only loves my money.

But her money made them a perfect match. He got what he wanted. She got what she wanted—was that so wrong?

Frustrated, she slapped the bed with her other hand. "Why did he have to come here and ruin everything?"

Brenda stood. "Stay here."

She threw on a silk robe and stormed downstairs.

She found Phil in the kitchen, peering into the refrigerator.

"You're a bastard, you know that?" she asked.

"Is there anything to eat in this place?"

"Do you hear me? I said you're a *bastard*. You think you can waltz in here—"

He closed the door and stared into her eyes, his face close to hers. "I don't *think*, I *know*. And stop being so dramatic. Get rid of the pool boy, and let's have some dinner."

Brenda could feel the blood rising to her cheeks. "I can't even count your mistresses on one hand! Why can't you let me have my fun?"

"Because with me, it *is* just fun. I know how to handle things. You'll let that trash fill your head full of pretty lies about your sagging ass until you run out of money—"

Brenda saw white. Raising both fists, she flung herself at her husband.

"I hate you!"

Phil grabbed one wrist in mid-air and slapped her across the face with his other hand. She spun away, but, keeping his grip on her wrist, he jerked her back into his arms.

Roaring, she wrestled to escape. He grabbed her other wrist and spun her around. As she twirled, Brenda felt her head clip the refrigerator and saw stars.

"Hey!"

She heard the word, and then she was falling.

Everything went black.

"Brenda?"

Someone called her name. She felt a hand on her cheek,

tapping.

"Brenda?"

She opened her eyes. James knelt beside her. Eyes bouncing left and right, searching for a frame of reference, she realized she was on her kitchen floor.

"What happened?" she croaked. She tried to sit up, but the room began to spin.

"Phil attacked you."

"Phil?"

She gasped, her memory returning. *He'd made her so angry* she'd pounded on Phil with her fists. He'd grabbed her— her head hit the refrigerator—

"Where is he?" she asked.

James frowned and pointed past her. "He's there."

"Where?"

James helped her sit up, and she saw Phil's body. He lay on his stomach, with his body splayed on the floor beside her.

"Phil!"

On her hands and knees, she crawled to him. Her hand touched the back of his head, and she jerked away, something sticky grabbing at her fingers. That's when she noticed the blood on the floor.

"He's bleeding."

"Not anymore. He's dead."

"*Dead?*"

Brenda raised her hand to her mouth and then lowered it, disgusted at the thought of the blood touching her face.

"What happened?"

"He was attacking you. I grabbed the salt shaker."

She glanced toward the kitchen table where she knew a tall, heavy pewter salt and pepper shaker sat. She saw only the pepper. Her gaze fell to the ground near the table where the top of the salt shaker sat, separated from the base. Salt scattered across the floor.

"You hit him with it?"

He nodded. "He collapsed on you. I pulled you out from under him. I tried to wake you up. When you wouldn't open your eyes, I checked on him, but he wasn't breathing."

"Did you call an ambulance?"

James scowled. "Are you crazy? A woman, her lover, and her dead husband? They'd lock us up and throw away the key."

"They wouldn't know you and me—"

James rolled his eyes. "Come *on*. It wouldn't take a genius to suspect it. One glance at the bed..."

Brenda gasped. "My bank accounts..."

"What about them?"

Once Brenda started making a mental list of the ways the police could connect her to James, the list was endless. Phil had found out. She'd definitely left evidence behind.

"What are we going to do?" she asked.

"Does anyone know he's here?"

"No. I don't know. He wasn't *supposed* to be here."

"We could say we never saw him. Get rid of the body."

"Get rid of the body?"

Brenda dropped her head into her hands, and James put his arm around her. She realized he thought she was crying. She wasn't. She wanted to—felt like she should—but the tears wouldn't come.

Maybe I'm in shock.

"I'll do it. I'll take care of it," he said.

She looked up at him as a thought bounced through her brain.

He can't leave me. I have this on him. I know what he did. He can never leave me.

Nothing about leaving her life as she knew it behind bothered her. She didn't want it anymore. None of it.

A fresh start. I need a fresh start.

She took James' hand.

"We can't risk staying. We have to go far away. Leave the body, and we'll go. I'll empty the accounts, and we'll go to a country where they can't bring us back."

James had been nodding, agreeing with her, but he reversed and began to shake his head.

"No. We still have to get rid of the body. It will slow down any investigation. Give us time."

"No body, no crime," she whispered. She'd heard the line on television a million times.

"Exactly."

"Okay. You..." She looked at Phil and rested her hand on the small of his back for a moment. One last gesture of affection for the good times. "You figure out what to do with Phil. I'll go get packed up and move what money I can."

James nodded and stood, holding out a hand to help her to her feet. He kissed her on the forehead and turned to head downstairs.

"Where are you going?" she asked.

"I need tools. Bags—"

"Tools?" She shook her head. "No. Don't tell me. I don't want to know."

Brenda went upstairs and packed. She used her laptop to move money into her personal account. She'd move more later. She didn't want things to look too suspicious, too fast. Her head throbbed. She lay on the bed and thought about the things she'd be leaving behind.

Maybe if I just close my eyes for a moment...

"Brenda?"

She opened her eyes and realized she must have fallen asleep.

"James?"

She sat up.

"It's done," he said.

She stood and followed him downstairs. The kitchen looked the same as it always did, no sign of Phil, no sign of blood.

"How?"

James ran his hand through his hair and offered her a sheepish smile. He was sweaty.

Why is he sweaty?

"I'm not saying it's perfect, but no one would know something happened here if they weren't *looking* for it. If somebody just walked in, they'd never know—"

"Darla!" Brenda blurted, her hand moving to her mouth.

"Who's Darla?"

"My friend. I'd asked her to come here and help get the house ready for the season."

"She's coming *here*? When?"

"Soon. A couple days."

"Call her. Cancel."

"But you said no one could tell. And won't it look suspicious if I cancel?"

James paced. Brenda moved as well and, in doing so, noticed three large dark green trash bags next to the sink.

"Is that—"

"Don't look at them," said James.

"What are you going to do with those?"

"Bury them, I guess."

"Where?"

"I don't know, Brenda!"

Brenda jumped. James had never screamed at her before. He might not be the perfect boyfriend, but like a good little gold-digger, he was exceedingly kind and patient.

He took a deep breath. "I'm sorry. This is stressful."

"I know."

Brenda's phone rang, and she froze, unsure of what to do.

She looked at the screen.

"Speak of the devil. It's Darla."

"Maybe she's calling to cancel."

Brenda answered the phone.

"Hello?"

"Hey, Brenda, it's Darla."

"Hello, Darla. How are you?" Talking to her Tennessee friend, she could hear her own accent thickening.

"Great. We're all really looking forward to the trip. Thank you so much for thinking of me—"

"My pleasure. You're doing me the favor." She looked at James and rolled her eyes. "But you know, I was thinking about canceling with you."

"Cancelling? Why?"

"Um, we were thinking maybe we'd just sell this place as is."

"Oh, Brenda, you *can't.* I promised everyone. We can get you top dollar if we fix things up."

"Uh," Brenda stammered, unsure how hard to push for cancellation.

Darla continued. "We have to come. You won't be sorry. But I have one little thing I wanted to let you know—Mariska's sister Carolina is coming to the house a little early. I hope that's okay?"

"What?" Brenda winced, knowing she'd nearly shrieked the word. "When? Why?"

"The weather. That awful Midwest *weather.*"

"When will she be here?"

"*Here?* Are you at the house now?"

"At the...no. No, I'm home getting ready for a trip. I'm going to, uh, Mexico."

She looked at James, and they shrugged at each other.

"You and Phil?" asked Darla.

"Sure. Yes. Me and Phil."

"Oh that's great. I went to Cancun back in—"

"Darla, I'm sorry, when is her sister going to be here, I mean, *there*? At the house?"

"Her plane will be landing in a little bit. Maybe a couple of hours?"

"A couple of hours?" Brenda could feel the panic welling in her chest. "I have to go. I'm sorry. I'm really busy packing."

"What about Carolina?"

"I'll be sure to have the key under the mat for her."

"Oh, Brenda, that's *wonderful*. You don't mind?"

"No problem. I have to go."

"You have a good time—"

Brenda disconnected and looked at James.

"Her friend's sister's going to be here in a couple of hours."

His eyes bulged. "What?" He turned and looked at the bags. "I was going to bury them."

"We have to go. We can take them with us."

"To the airport?"

"We'll leave them in the car in the parking lot."

"That defeats the purpose. We need to *hide* the body. If we just leave his empty car at the airport, maybe they'll think he went somewhere."

"Ran away with a mistress," muttered Brenda.

"Yes, *good*," said James, pointing at her.

"What if we take the bags with us and bury them somewhere on the way?"

James shook his head. "Drive around with a body in the car in broad daylight? What if we get pulled over? And where exactly are we taking them?"

Brenda's gaze drifted to the kitchen counter, where she noticed something behind the coffee maker.

"What is that?" she asked. She stepped closer, squinting at the object.

"What?"

"Is that a *finger*?" she asked, her voice rising an octave.

James moved to see from her angle. He grunted something that sounded like *whoops*, pushed aside the coffee maker, and grabbed the finger. "It must have shot off when—"

"Don't finish that sentence." Brenda stumbled back and pulled a chair from the table to sit. She felt ill.

"Sorry. I thought I had it all." James pulled the trashcan out and tossed the finger inside.

"You're going to put it in there?"

"The other bags are tied tight already."

"But—"

"Tomorrow's trash day. No one will look in the bag. Don't worry about it."

"Don't worry about it." Brenda sighed. "We have to go. Carolina is going to be here in two hours. And believe me, she won't promise not to tell if she finds those bags here."

James put his hands on his hips. "Screw it. We'll get out of town and see how things shake out. You can tell people Phil went on vacation with you to buy us time and *then* say he's on a business trip or something. If people buy it and everything seems safe, we'll come back and deal with the body."

"But what does that mean? What are you going to do with the big bags *now*? You can't take *those* to the curb."

James took a deep breath, tilted back his head to stare at the ceiling, and released the trapped air through his nose.

"I have an idea."

CHAPTER THIRTY

Charlotte had never seen women pack so fast in her life. Mariska and Darla were standing by the front door with their suitcases at their feet five minutes after Declan let it slip that Phil was "living" in the attic.

"Let's go!" yelled Darla as she dropped her bag at the door.

Carolina toddled from the kitchen, dragging a trash bag full of frozen meat behind her.

"I couldn't leave the meat."

The three ladies dragged their belongings to the bus and sat there while the cops spoke with the others.

"So, how long have you been collecting these bits?" said a police officer with blonde hair knotted at the nape of her neck. She scowled at the uncovered butter dish.

"Since the day we arrived," said Charlotte.

"Oh, you'll want this," said Seamus, opening a drawer and tossing the police woman a plastic bag he pulled from inside.

She scowled. "What is this?"

"Junk I found in the kitchen pipes. Hair, grease, fat—"

The officer grimaced and dropped the bag on the counter as if it were scalding.

"You found all this and only *now* thought to call us?" she

asked.

"The storm would have made it impossible for you to get here." Charlotte's voice trailed to silence. Even as she said the words, she began to second-guess their *we'll call the police when the storm leaves* idea. Maybe a finger and an ear *were* worth a ringy-dingy to the local constabulary.

Behind her, a gasping sob rang out. They'd called over Emmitt to confirm the semi-transparent reflection they'd spotted in the photo was James. The moment he'd seen his ex-boyfriend's familiar t-shirt, he'd burst into tears.

"James is a graphic designer," he said, sobbing as they showed him the doctored photos of Phil.

Dinah took a break from consoling Emmitt and strolled to Charlotte's side.

"So this is all about James and that woman, right?" she mumbled, holding her hand in front of her mouth to keep the police from reading her lips.

Charlotte nodded.

"I *told* Emmitt that James had propositioned me." Clearly pleased she'd been proven right, Dinah smiled and worked her way back to Emmitt. "He was never good enough for you, dear," she said, patting him on the back.

He sobbed louder.

Once the police had gathered the facts and the process of removing Phil from the attic had begun, the rest of the Pineapple Port crew piled into *The Reptile*. They'd been asked to stay in town another day while the police sorted things out.

Seamus hopped in the driver's seat, and they roared away from the beach house.

"I hope the ice machine at the motel is full," said Carolina, eyeballing her bag of meat.

"I hope the police will let us go tomorrow so we can get home in time for Thanksgiving. I'm afraid they suspect *we* were involved," said Mariska.

"It probably didn't help that we were driving around in a snake," said Carolina as they pulled into the driveway of a cheap beach hotel. The one good thing to come of the debacle was off-season rates.

"It probably didn't help that we didn't call the police right away, even if they *couldn't* get to the house," said Charlotte.

"Or that we'd felt comfortable enough to live in a house with severed body parts," added Declan.

Darla raised her hands and flopped them back into her lap. "Frank is never going to let me hear the end of this. A sheriff's wife accepting an invitation from a killer and then handling *everything* wrong,"

As the bus pulled to a stop, Bob stood, smiling.

"What are you so happy about?" asked Mariska.

"We finally get a real vacation," said Bob.

Chuck grinned. "Yeah. This place might not be fancy, but at least they won't ask us to paint it."

~~ THE END ~~

Want more? FREE PREVIEW!

If you liked this book, read on for a preview of the next Pineapple Port Mystery AND the Shee McQueen Mystery-Thriller Series (which shares characters with the Pineapple Port world!).

Thank you!

Thank you for reading! If you enjoyed this book, please swing back to Amazon and leave me a review — even short reviews help authors like me find new fans!

ABOUT THE AUTHOR

USA Today and *Wall Street Journal* bestselling author Amy Vansant has written over 30 books, including the fun, thrilling Shee McQueen series, the rollicking, twisty Pineapple Port Mysteries, and the action-packed Kilty urban fantasies. She's also the founder of AuthorsXP.com – a site for authors (marketing help) and readers (free and deal books!).

Amy lives in Jupiter, Florida, with her muse/husband and a goony Bordoodle named Archer.

http://www.AmyVansant.com

FOLLOW AMY on AMAZON or BOOKBUB

Books by Amy Vansant

__Pineapple Port Mysteries__
Funny, clean & full of unforgettable characters
__Shee McQueen Mystery-Thrillers__
Action-packed, fun romantic mystery-thrillers
__Kilty Urban Fantasy/Romantic Suspense__
Action-packed romantic suspense/urban fantasy
__Slightly Romantic Comedies__
Classic romantic romps
__The Magicatory__
Middle-grade fantasy

FREE PREVIEW

PINEAPPLE

DISCO

A Pineapple Port Mystery: Book Six – By
Amy Vansant

Chapter One

It started with the brush of a hand.

Every day Gloria walked the River Walk, not far from her new beach apartment. After falling into a little money, she'd left the Pineapple Port retirement community for the cool beach breezes of the Gulf.

Gloria enjoyed nodding her head and smiling at the people who passed in the opposite direction when she walked. She liked everything about her new lifestyle by the water, but she especially enjoyed the walks.

Walking kept her need to *right wrongs* at bay.

She hadn't slashed a tire, or dropped a bug in a cocktail, or switched yard decorations between neighbors with competing gnome ideologies, in nearly three months.

Even Superman grew old and let a few offenses slide here and there, didn't he?

Gloria let her mind wander when she walked. She waved at dogs and called them *buddy,* or *sweetie* if they had a bow or a pink collar. She liked the Yorkie terrier with the watery eyes and the regal standard poodle that ran at the same graceful pace as her owner. The owner never smiled, but the dog's presence said she wasn't a bad person and Gloria believed the dog.

Thanks to the poodle, I let sourpuss off the hook. 'Old Gloria' never would have let that skinny woman's refusal to return a smile slide. I'm maturing.

Her patience had limits, of course. Gloria did *not* like the two ladies who hogged the whole sidewalk and never deigned to step aside for her to pass. *She* had to balance-beam the curb, or tumble into the bike lane to avoid being clipped by their stupid rounded shoulders. Those ladies...

Those ladies didn't deserve a pass.

After the fifth or sixth offense, Gloria followed them home. One had a New England Patriots football flag flying outside her house, so Gloria returned under cover of night to replace it with a Miami Dolphins flag. The next time she passed the women she made a point to *not* move out of their way. As they jostled to avoid knocking into her she shouted, "*Go Dolphins!*"

After that day, the women fell single file when they saw her coming. They knew *she* knew where they lived. Gloria had a giant bottle of vinegar for the other woman's manicured lawn, should they forget their manners.

See how she likes the word MOVE scrawled across her front yard in brown, dead grass.

Other than those two sidewalk-hogging, boorish wenches, Gloria liked the people and pets on her walk. She liked the chubby Italian man who waddled along yammering on his phone in his native tongue. She liked the woman who always wore too many clothes, but never appeared sweaty.

Classy.

Most of all, she liked the tanned man with the dark hair. He always flashed his perfect smile and winked. She didn't know if he wore dentures or had those replacement teeth people had drilled into their jaw bones, but his chompers were *impressive.* Nearly as striking as the cowlick in his magnificent mane of dark hair. The front row of follicles stood strong and proud, like a hair wave begging to be surfed.

I never properly appreciated men's hair until I grew older and suddenly none of the men have any. Think of all the hair I took for granted as a foolish young girl...

The man had kind eyes, and those sparkling orbs always found hers. At first, she'd thought the man was just friendly. After his walk she imagined he returned to a pretty wife sipping coffee on her lanai with a good book propped on her lap. But then she noticed he didn't wear a wedding ring. Not even the telltale tan line of a cheater. If he was a widower, he'd been one for some time.

The man's smile and wink were soon accompanied by a nod, the tip of an invisible hat, and once, what she felt sure was a blush.

Mornings changed. Gloria grew giddy pre-walk, eager to see Smiley Joe, which is what she'd started calling the man in her head.

Then it happened.

As she passed Smiley Joe on the narrow pathway, his hand brushed hers.

Gloria gasped and kept walking. After a dozen steps she glanced back, but Joe had continued on his way.

After that day, he *always* touched her hand. Anticipating the contact, her hand began to jerk away from her body, reaching to feel his, as if it had a mind of its own. Their touches became more eager. On day six their pinkies intertwined and uncoiled, slipping away like lovesick garden snakes as they continued in their opposite directions.

Then it happened. Smiley Joe wore his usual white t-shirt, but he'd handwritten *Hi* on the chest. She'd been so shocked to see the word she'd forgotten to reach for his hand.

Was that message for me?

The next day he wore a new t-shirt. She assumed it was

new—it had looked as though the previous day's *Hi* was written in permanent marker and she couldn't imagine how he could have washed it out.

Now, his shirt said *Will.*

Gloria knew the messages on his shirts were for her. His eyes were playful. Twinkling with mischief.

He's a scamp.

On the third day, the shirt said *You.*

Gloria felt a rush of excitement.

It's a question! He's asking me a question on his shirt, one word per day.

The mornings became almost impossible to manage. She didn't want to leave too soon and miss meeting him at the spot they passed every day. She didn't know how far he walked before they met each other. Leave too soon and he might miss her entirely. Same applied to leaving too late. She had to wait until the exact right moment, 7:39 a.m. This grew increasingly difficult, because she kept waking up earlier and earlier, eager to see what his next word would be.

It was *Go.*

Hi Will You Go.

Gloria had new problems to consider. Would she recognize when the sentence was over? Would he remember to punctuate the last word with a question mark? Would the last tee feature *only* a question mark? And then what? If it was a question—and she assumed it was—how would she answer? Would she write it on *her* shirt with permanent marker? Should she go shopping for a cheap tee she didn't mind ruining with ink?

The next word was *Out.*

No punctuation.

Gloria didn't want to be presumptuous, but she felt confident she'd guessed the rest of his mysterious missive. Her day would soon arrive.

What if I accept his invitation and the message isn't for me?

If she wore a cheap tee with *Yes* written on it and he ignored her, she would just *die*.

The next day he smiled and winked with *With* on his tee. The day after that, *Me*.

Still no punctuation. She knew she had one more day. The question mark would be the next day. Or not. Maybe he'd forget to add punctuation.

Can I date a man who doesn't properly punctuate? So many questions...

Gloria drove to *Bealls* and bought a cheap white tee. It took nearly an hour to decide on the color of the marker. She'd had no idea they came in so many colors. Back in her day, permanent markers came in one color: black.

Period.

Or maybe red, too...but certainly not green and purple and...

She chose a feminine hot pink and hoped it didn't come off trashy.

She spent another two hours picking the size of the lettering and contemplating cursive versus block and all caps versus first letter capitalization only.

On Thursday, Smiley Joe walked by with a huge question mark on his shirt.

His other words had been in black, but the question mark glowed in hot pink, just like her *Yes* tee back home on her kitchen table.

It's as if we're meant to be together.

Gloria barely slept Thursday night. Her mind raced with anticipation and questions.

Should I add an exclamation point to the end of Yes? Would that be too forward?

Friday morning, she donned her block lettering, first-letter-cap, no punctuation, *Yes* tee and leapt from her car as if it were a circus cannon instead of a Mercedes. She adjusted her pace to keep from speed-walking to her destiny.

Gloria practiced holding people's gazes as she walked. She didn't want to hold Smiley Joe's attention too long and look desperate, but she didn't want him to wonder if her shirt was for him. Or maybe she did. If it seemed as if the question *hadn't* been for her, she wanted the opportunity to look away and keep walking, as if she always wore a tee with a giant pink *Yes* on it.

As she approached the portion of the walk where they always met, she could barely breathe.

It wasn't until she reached the corner that she realized he wasn't there.

She leaned forward, expecting to see him at any moment.

He never appeared.

On the drive back to her apartment, Gloria felt like a deflated balloon.

Where was he? Had he fallen ill? Twisted an ankle?

Maybe someone else had answered him?

No.

She *knew* the shirts had been for her.

After much hemming and hawing, she wore the *Yes* tee again the next day.

Again, he didn't show.

Something horrible had happened. Gloria was sure of it.

She needed a detective to find Smiley Joe.

She   needed   to   call   Charlotte.

Chapter Two

Two Weeks Previous

Stephanie yawned into her hand and read the plaques on the wall of the bar for the fifth time.

Free beers tomorrow.

You can't drink all day if you don't start in the morning.

Wish you were beer.

She flicked a peanut across the bar top.

Nothing about this is right.

Assassins of her caliber weren't meant to spend time drinking terrible iced tea while watching teenagers peddle drugs on the corner.

This is Declan's fault.

She'd allowed herself to be inspired by her ex-boyfriend's inherently good nature. She missed him, and her usual charms had ceased to sway his affections her way. In an attempt to better resemble his *new* little Ms. Perfect Girlfriend, Charlotte, she'd decided to *pull a Dexter* and only kill people who deserved it.

It turned out being good was even more boring than she'd feared.

She'd *barely* refrained from killing the neighbor who reported her to her community association for not recycling. She was hiding behind the woman's bedroom door, knife in hand, when it hit her: *People aren't supposed to murder people for being bitchy.*

It was a close call. If the woman hadn't forgotten to brush her teeth Stephanie might have had to exterminate the tattle-telling little rat just to get out of the woman's rat-hole undetected.

No, she didn't trust her ability to identify *people who deserved to die* versus *people who are too annoying to live,* so she decided to pick a ham-handedly obvious target.

A drug dealer.

I should win some sort of serial killer Oscar for the restraint I've shown.

Not only was she hunting a drug dealer, but she was hunting the top banana. By sunrise, she could have easily taken out three or four of the hoppers on the corner, but she didn't. She could hear Declan in her head... *They probably had lousy home lives and fell in with the wrong crowd and blah blah bleeding heart blah...*

Stephanie knew Declan wouldn't give her any credit for killing a kid who made bad life choices.

She could have killed the slick-haired man who brought the corner kids their supply, but she didn't.

Instead, she decided next time the drop-off man showed up, she'd track *that* guy back to the biggest, *baddest* guy.

That meant a lot of surveillance; the most boring part of killing.

This is all my mother's fault.

Why did her mother have to pass down the serial killer gene? The time she wasted hunting, dreaming about hunting—she could have started a second business. Learned another language. Learned to cook soufflés...*something.*

The neighbor she nearly killed had a basket of knitting supplies. She'd stared at it for some time from her hiding spot behind the bedroom door. It seemed like such a peaceful hobby.

Why can't I love knitting?

Instead, she'd mulled using the knitting needle to kill the woman just to make her attack a little more sporting.

Maybe it wasn't *all* her mother's fault. Sure, her mother was the most prolific serial killer of all time—whether the world knew it or not—but her mother had also abandoned her as a baby. Wasn't that supposed to mess up kids? Maybe she was just like those hoppers on the corner out there. A tough life filled with bad decisions.

Or, it could have been the Honey Badgers. They certainly encouraged the bloodlust in her. Working for that barely sanctioned drug task force was where she learned how to kill and also where she realized how much she *liked* it. The Honey Badgers were like *21 Jump Street* and *Training Day* had spawned a nightmare baby. What if she hadn't joined? Maybe she'd be married with three kids and head of the PTA.

Stephanie chuckled at the thought.

Maybe the Honey Badgers had done her a favor.

She glanced to the left to keep tabs on the cop sitting in the corner of the bar.

Still nursing his beer.

She'd seen him before, but realized he posed no threat. He wore his badge, but he didn't *feel* like a cop. She never saw him do anything *coppy*. During her time in surveillance purgatory she'd seen a thug rough up a kid right outside the bar window. The cop hadn't moved. Hadn't even feigned interest.

Something's off with him.

Maybe he's lousy at being a cop. Lazy. Maybe when he was off duty, he was *off duty*. Though if he liked separation, spending his evenings sitting at the one bar with a clear view of the area's worst drug dealing corner seemed like a bad spot to hole up while wearing a cop badge.

"You want another?" asked the bartender.

Stephanie licked her lips, considering. Maybe it was time to pack it in for the evening. It seemed the drug trade was suffering a lull and—

"It's on me," said a voice to her left.

A man sat two stools down from Stephanie.

The cop.

"You don't look like you belong here," he added, smiling.

She surveyed the stranger. He was a handsome man for his age—maybe sixty something. He didn't look grizzled enough to be a cop who hung out in filthy dive bars during his down time.

"Neither do you."

The cop pulled his light jacket a little tighter, covering his badge. "I've seen you before."

The bartender put another iced tea in front of Stephanie and she cringed. The tea was terrible. She couldn't even imagine what a person could do to ice tea to make it taste that bad. She didn't like to drink during a hunt, but it occurred to her a glass of bourbon might be required to kill whatever was living in the tea.

The cop nodded toward her glass. "In the program?"

She laughed. "Right. Maybe I came to this nasty bar for the aesthetics. What better place to sober up?"

He shook his head. "No. I didn't think you came here not to drink. I think you came here to watch *them*." His eyes flicked in the direction of the dealers outside.

Stephanie frowned. "Do you have a point?"

Shaking his head, the cop stood to pull two dollars from his wallet. He put the money on the bar.

"I don't know what you're up to, but be careful."

Stephanie arched an eyebrow, amused. "Back at you."

The cop left and Stephanie watched him go, allowing her attention to drift to the men standing on the corner outside. *Men.* They were barely more than boys. She checked her watch. It was ten p.m. Last time their supplier had appeared at ten seventeen to gather cash and replace drugs. She needed to prepare to tail him.

Stephanie put a few more dollar bills on the counter.

"Thanks. I'll send you the bill for the stomach pump."

Eyes fixed on his newspaper, the bartender replied without missing a beat. "Try the shrimp cocktail next time if that's your thing."

Stephanie headed outside, walking briskly towards the junker car she'd rented for keeping a low profile in the neighborhood. Her long blonde hair tucked beneath a baseball cap, she'd worn baggy clothing to cover the rest of her impressive assets. She strode down the street affecting masculine gait so as not to shine like a beacon of weakness.

As she passed an alley, an arm hooked around her waist, jerking her into the shadows. Stephanie struck with the back of her fist, connecting with the attacker's windpipe. She heard him gasp. His arm slipped from her waist, but not before she saw a flash of movement to her left, too far away to be the same enemy. She felt the sharp crack of something striking her skull. From the pain, she guessed a ballpeen hammer.

The world spun and everything went black.

Her final thought was that her last meal had been that *revolting* ice tea.

Get *Pineapple Disco* on Amazon!

ANOTHER FREE PREVIEW!

THE GIRL WHO WANTS

A Shee McQueen Mystery-Thriller by Amy Vansant

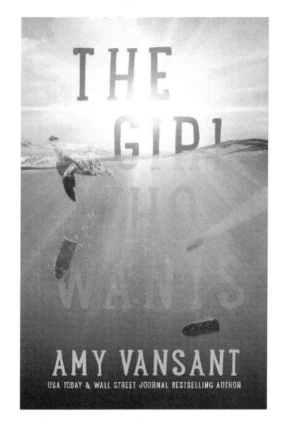

Chapter One

Three Weeks Ago, Nashua, New Hampshire.

Shee realized her mistake the moment her feet left the grass.

He's enormous.

She'd watched him drop from the side window of the house. He landed four feet from where she stood, and still her brain refused to register the warning signs. The nose, big and lumpy as breadfruit, the forehead some beach town could use as a jetty if they buried him to his neck...

His knees bent to absorb his weight, and *her* brain thought, *got you.*

Her brain couldn't be bothered with simple math: *Giant, plus Shee, equals Pain.*

Instead, she jumped to tackle him, dangling airborne as his knees straightened and the *pet the rabbit* bastard stood to his full height.

Crap.

The math added up pretty quickly after that.

Hovering like Superman mid-flight, there wasn't much she could do to change her disastrous trajectory. She'd *felt* like a superhero when she left the ground. Now, she felt more like a Canada goose staring into the propellers of Captain Sully's Airbus A320.

She might take down the plane, but it was going to *hurt.*

Frankenjerk turned toward her at the same moment she plowed into him. She clamped her arms around his waist like a little girl hugging a redwood. Lurch returned the embrace, twisting her to the ground. Her back hit the dirt, and air burst from her lungs like a double shotgun blast.

Ow.

Wheezing, she punched upward, striking Beardless Hagrid in the throat.

That didn't go over well.

Grabbing her shoulder with one hand, Dickasaurus flipped her on her stomach like a sausage link, slipped his hand under her chin, and pressed his forearm against her windpipe.

The only air she'd gulped before he cut her supply stank of damp armpit. He'd tucked her cranium in his arm crotch, much like the famous noggin-less horseman once held his severed head. Fireworks exploded in the dark behind her eyes.

That's when a thought occurred to her.

I haven't been home in fifteen years.

What if she died in Gigantor's armpit? Would her father even know?

Has it really been that long?

Flopping like a landed fish, she forced her assailant to adjust his hold and sucked a breath as she flipped on her back. Spittle glistened on his lips, his brow furrowed as if she'd asked him to read a paragraph of big-boy words.

His nostrils flared like the Holland Tunnel.

There's an idea.

Making a V with her fingers, Shee thrust upward, stabbing into his nose, straining to reach his tiny brain.

Goliath roared. Jerking back, he grabbed her arm to unplug her fingers from his nose socket. She whipped away her limb before he had a good grip, fearing he'd snap her bones with his Godzilla paws.

Kneeling before her, he clamped both hands over his face, cursing as blood seeped from behind his fingers.

Shee's gaze didn't linger on that mess. Her focus fell to his crotch, hovering a foot above her feet, protected by nothing but a thin pair of oversized sweatpants.

Scrambled eggs, sir?

She kicked.

He howled.

Shee scuttled back like a crab, found her feet, and

snatched her gun from her side. The gun she should have pulled *before* trying to tackle the Empire State Building.

"Move a muscle, and I'll aerate you," she said. She always liked that line.

The golem growled but remained on the ground like a good dog, cradling his family jewels.

Shee's partner in this manhunt, a local cop easier on the eyes than he was useful, rounded the corner and drew his own weapon.

She smiled and holstered the gun he'd lent her. Unknowingly.

"Glad you could make it."

Her portion of the operation accomplished, she headed toward the car as more officers swarmed the scene.

"Shee, where are you going?" called the cop.

She stopped and turned.

"Home, I think."

His gaze dropped to her hip.

"Is that my gun?"

Get *The Girl Who Wants* on Amazon!

Made in United States
Troutdale, OR
11/09/2023

14438561R00122